DEAD RINGER

AN ANNABELLE ARCHER WEDDING PLANNER
MYSTERY NOVELLA

LAURA DURHAM

BROADMOOR BOOKS

To Emma,
my novelist-in-training and this book's first beta reader

A glamorous bridal show. A sophisticated jewelry heist. Can Annabelle track down the baubles and nab a burglar? Wedding planner Annabelle Archer knows that the only thing as crazy as a wedding day is a bridal show. When DC's most stylish bridal showcase is disrupted by a jewelry heist and a quarter of a million dollars worth of diamond rings disappear, Annabelle and her team are determined to find the bling to help the jeweler and save the show. One problem: the jewelry was stolen during a blackout and no one saw a thing. With the clock counting down to show time, Annabelle and her sassy assistant, Kate, must hunt for a sophisticated jewel thief and unravel a clever caper.

CHAPTER 1

"**W**here are you?" I asked, holding my phone against my ear and carrying a pair of overstuffed canvas bags in my other hand. The hotel elevator had deposited me on the basement level of the W Hotel and I side-stepped cardboard boxes, bolts of gold sequined fabric, and bright orange buckets of flowers as I made my way to the ballroom.

"We're in the middle section about halfway down," Kate's voice crackled through the phone. The W Hotel sat right across from the White House, and I wondered if this had anything to do with the dodgy cell reception or if it was merely a basement issue.

The modern hotel had once been one of the oldest historic hotels in the city, the Hotel Washington, but after declining for many years, had been snapped up by a ritzy hotel group and refashioned into a sleek W Hotel. The classic lobby with brocade settees had been replaced by the Living Room with a black-and-white tile floor, a 360-degree bar that pumped out club music, and a virtual fireplace projected onto a flat screen. The rooftop, with its impressive open-air view of the White House and frequent sightings of the president's helicopter detail, had become a highly selective spot for cocktails, featuring willowy women in skimpy black dresses as gatekeepers. I never felt quite hip enough to be at the W.

"Okay, I'll see you in a second." I slipped my phone into the pocket of my jeans and shifted one of the heavy bags to my now-free hand. I stepped carefully down the staircase that led from the elevator bank to the ballroom level, avoiding the lighting crew on tall ladders at the bottom. Almost every inch of the floor was covered in boxes, crates, or tables yet to be unfolded.

"A bridal show is even more chaotic than a wedding," I muttered to myself as I snaked a path through the ballroom foyer. And as the owner of one of Washington DC's top wedding planning firms, I knew firsthand how chaotic weddings could be. I passed through the propped-open double doors to the ballroom and peered across the room, which had already been divided into thirds with panels of ivory fabric that reached from floor to ceiling. A pair of modern crystal chandeliers shaped like massive, glittering cones dominated the ceiling in the long rectangular space and drew my eyes away from the set-up clutter covering the dark carpet. I spotted my assistant's blond bob about halfway down the center, as promised. She waved at me with both hands and what appeared to be a to-go coffee in each one.

"I hope one of those is for me," I said to Kate, dropping the bags on the floor once I'd maneuvered across the room to reach her.

She held out a cup ringed in a brown cardboard holder. "The Annabelle Archer signature drink: a mocha with mint."

"You're the best." I took a sip and let the warmth and caffeine do their work. "But you know that not every person needs a signature drink." Sometimes the signature drinks and custom signage and personalized details that had taken over the wedding world were too much for me.

"Well, you've got one," she said. "And I've got doughnuts behind the bar."

"District Doughnuts?"

She grinned at me. "Yep. The cinnamon sugar ones."

My stomach growled, reminding me that I hadn't eaten breakfast yet. I glanced at the eight-foot-long gold bar with mercury glass panels set against the tall fabric wall. A white-framed mirror with our Wedding Belles logo painted in gold on the reflective surface hung in the middle of the drape.

"You're sure about the bar?" I asked as I ducked behind it to search for the box of doughnuts. Kate had convinced me that instead of a tablescape like all the other DC wedding planners would do for their display, we should have a bar. Even though I'd started Wedding Belles five years ago and was no longer considered the new kid on the block, I still wasn't completely comfortable being a trailblazer.

I found the white box, grabbed a doughnut, and took a bite. The cinnamon sugar atop the warm cake doughnut made me glad I'd skipped breakfast. Not that I'd had any food worth eating in my apartment.

"Of course I'm sure. What bride doesn't want to belly up to a bar?" Kate hopped up onto one of the ornate gold bar stools and crossed her legs, exposing most of her legs as her black miniskirt slid up her thighs. Most people wore jeans and T-shirts to setup but Kate considered every time she stepped out of her apartment as an opportunity to meet Mr. Right. Hence the miniskirt, snug red sweater, and full makeup. I actually had to think hard to remember if I'd put on mascara after throwing my long auburn hair up into a ponytail this morning.

"Frankly, I'm hoping for sober brides." Richard walked up and gave me a peck on the cheek. "It would be a nice change."

"You're only saying that because our last drunk bride got up on the stage and started rapping as the band was breaking down," Kate said.

He shuddered. "Girls that white should never rap."

"Doughnut?" I offered and motioned to the box.

Richard shook his head. "I don't need sugar all over my shirt."

He picked at a piece of non-existent lint on his crisp lavender button-down shirt. Richard was another one who didn't do jeans and T-shirts for setup.

Richard was the owner of Richard Gerard Catering, one of the top caterers in the city, and had been my go-to caterer and best friend since I'd hit the wedding planner scene. Richard prided himself on impeccable taste and was a stickler for good behavior. I was amazed he'd survived in weddings as long as he had.

"Where are you set up?" I asked, giving a cursory glance around. From the pile of foliage on one side of me and the glass case on the other, it seemed like we were between a jeweler and a florist but, I didn't see a catering setup.

Richard swept a hand through his spiky brown hair and motioned behind the drape wall. "I'm on the dark side of the moon."

I patted his back. "I'm sure it won't be so bad once all the lighting is on."

"You must be out of your mind, Annabelle. Anyone who's anyone is in the center."

"I'm sure that's not true," I said.

Richard narrowed his eyes at Kate. "Who did you flirt with to land a space in the middle of the room?"

"Hey," Kate said in her affronted tone. "I'll have you know that the show staff is all women."

"And Kate would never use her feminine wiles to get us a better spot in the show," I said with more conviction than I felt.

"Thank you," Kate said, then put a hand over her mouth and lowered her voice. "But you know I'd take one for the team if they had a hot guy in charge."

I nodded even though I didn't think flirting with an attractive man was the strict definition of "taking one for the team." Especially since I couldn't seem to *stop* her from flirting with hot guys.

Richard lowered his voice to a hiss. "I have a cosmetic dentist next to me."

"What's wrong with dentists?" Kate asked. "I've dated several nice ones. They make good money." Kate probably knew the average salary of every man she met off the top of her head.

Richard tapped one foot on the carpet. "Nothing. Unless you're trying to convince people to sample your crème brulee tartlets and profiteroles wrapped in spun sugar."

I could see his point. Sugar was a hard sell next to photos of yellowed teeth.

He began fidgeting with one of his silver cuff links. "The only thing worse would be someone next to me offering on-site colonics."

Kate put her cup down on the bar. "And I'm done with the coffee."

"Brides are coming here to drink Champagne and eat cake," I said. "They want to indulge. And no one can say no to your brownie meringue pops."

Richard allowed himself a tiny smile. "Of course they can't. Those babies are like heaven." He gave me a quick hug. "You always know what to say."

"That's what they tell me." I'd honed my skill of calming down skittish brides and their nervous mothers by being the voice of reason for my neurotic colleagues.

"Well, I'd better return to my side before those dental assistants run out of sugar-free gum and start eyeing my sweets display." He disappeared around the corner of the drape.

I stepped back and gave our bare bar a once-over. "Speaking of setting up . . ."

"Don't worry." Kate slid off the bar stool. "Buster and Mack promised to drape the rose gold branches over our bar for us."

I gaped at the huge pile of leafy, spray-painted tree branches that nearly covered the floor next to us. "Is all of that for us?"

"Not all of it. Buster and Mack are using some of it. The canopy will cover both of our displays."

"So the Mighty Morphins will be next to us?" Buster and

Mack's flower shop was called Lush, but everyone called them the Mighty Morphin Flower Arrangers.

Kate nodded. "Isn't it going to be fun?"

I sipped my warm mocha, then took a bite of doughnut. Kate was right, I thought. We were hanging out with our friends, we were stocked up on sugar, and we didn't need to get anyone down the aisle. Today was going to be fun.

"Annabelle!" I heard my name shrieked across the room. Fern, short for Fernando, was headed my way. He'd pulled his dark hair up in a man bun and wore a velvet-green smoking jacket with a green and yellow paisley ascot. No one could say that DC's top hairstylist didn't make a statement.

"Thank heavens you're here," he said when he reached me. His breath was ragged from either exertion or hysteria.

"What's wrong?" I asked.

He pressed a hand to his chest. "I can't work under these conditions. It's a disaster."

"Take a breath." I led him over to a bar stool to sit down. "What do you need me to do?"

"I'm so glad you asked." Fern collapsed onto a stool and peered at me from under the arm he'd slung across his eyes. "You and Kate are so good at organizing. I need you to help me stage a coup."

So much for our fun day.

CHAPTER 2

"**A**nd who are we overthrowing today?" I asked Fern as he fanned himself with a monogrammed handkerchief he'd produced from the breast pocket of his smoking jacket.

"Christopher."

Kate tilted her head to one side. "Who's Christopher?"

"Exactly." Fern pointed at her. "Who is he? Why is he here? Why do I have to work with another hairstylist for the fashion show?"

Things began to click into place for me. "So you're doing the models' hair for the fashion show?"

Fern flung the handkerchief over his face and tilted back on the bar stool. "Of course. I always do the hair for the show. Alone."

"And now you have to work with another stylist." Fern didn't like to share the spotlight with anyone so double billing on the biggest bridal show of the year could push him over the edge.

He peeked at me from underneath the handkerchief. "Not just another stylist, Annabelle. A newbie. A nobody."

Kate rolled her eyes. Talking Fern off of the ledge was nothing new for either of us.

"But you're the senior stylist, right?" Kate asked. "The veteran must be the one to call the shots."

"Veteran?" Fern let the handkerchief fall off his face as he sat up. "That makes me sound so old and . . ." He raised an eyebrow and grinned. "So butch."

"You know what Kate means." I sat down on the stool next to him. "You can use your wealth of experience to guide him. Be a mentor."

Fern shook his head. "Too late. He's taken over and changed my entire style concept for the show."

Kate leaned one elbow on the gold bar. "How did that happen? Do the show directors know?"

It was hard to imagine a personality as forceful as Fern's getting steamrolled into anything. Even the most hardened bridezilla became putty in his hands once he told them to sit down and be quiet. It was a transformation I relished watching, even though I knew I could never get away with talking to brides the way he did. He was famous for lovingly calling his brides tramps and hussies, and they adored him for it. I had a pretty good feeling that I would be fired if I attempted the same tactics.

Fern nodded, then picked up his handkerchief from his lap and dabbed at his eyes. "They'll go along with anything this Christopher suggests."

Kate expression told me that she felt as perplexed as I did. Something wasn't right about this story. Fern was a legend in the wedding-hair world and had been doing the hair for this bridal show for years.

"What aren't you telling us?" I asked

"It's too horrible." Fern pressed his fingers to his mouth. "I can't say it. You'll have to meet him."

What could possibly be so terrible that Fern couldn't even say it out loud? Before I could press him further, Kate looked over my shoulder and gasped. I spun around on the bar stool and saw what had caused her mouth to drop open. Diamonds.

The jeweler next to us was putting the finishing touches on a glittering display of engagement rings inside a waist-high wood and glass case. The rings lay on cushioned black-velvet trays in perfect rows. A stack of cream-colored business cards sat on top of the case along with a bunch of pink roses bursting out of an opaque white vase shaped like a fish bowl. A sign that read "Goodman & Sons" in black swirling letters hung behind the display.

The petite dark-haired woman who'd been arranging the rings slid the glass door to the back of the case closed and locked it with a small key. She glanced up and started when she saw Kate gaping at her.

"Sorry," I said. "My associate can't help ogling your diamonds."

Fern whipped around in his stool, his tears seeming to dry instantly. "Diamonds?"

"You're welcome to look," the woman said.

She didn't need to tell Kate or Fern twice. In mere seconds, they both were leaning over the case. I slid down from my stool and joined them.

"I'm Annabelle. I own Wedding Belles."

"I know." The woman took the hand I held out. "I'm Lorinda Goodman. We met at the Hay-Adams Hotel's Love Brunch."

As soon as she said her name I remembered sitting next to her at the annual wedding planner's party. She'd told me about the jewelry shop she'd taken over from her father because, despite the company name, he'd never had any sons. At the brunch her long dark hair had been down, but now she wore it pulled back in a bun at the nape of her neck.

"Of course," I said. "I thought you looked familiar. How funny that we ended up next to each other today."

Lorinda smiled as she walked out from behind the display case. "I have to thank you, actually. You're the reason I'm doing the show. You said such great things about it that I signed up."

"Well, I hope it goes well for you. The brides who come here are usually well-qualified." That was wedding lingo that meant they could afford luxury items like big diamonds and pricey wedding planners.

"Excuse me, sweetie." Fern took Lorinda's hand and led her back to the glass case. "How many carats is that one?"

Fern's love of big gemstones was almost as legendary as his reputation. He owned several rings with stones large enough to make waving an ordeal. Even now he wore a blue topaz ring larger than some robin's eggs.

Lorinda peered into the case. "The one in the middle? That's a three-carat cushion cut."

Kate and Fern both sighed and leaned in closer to the case.

"That would look gorgeous on me," Fern whispered to Kate, and she nodded.

"Do you want to try it on?" Lorinda asked.

Fern swooned against Kate and squeaked out a yes.

Lorinda unlocked the case and gently pulled out the sparkling ring. Fern slid it onto his right ring finger.

"It's perfection," he said.

I shook my head. "Shouldn't we be setting up, Kate, and shouldn't Fern be doing hair?"

Fern frowned at me. "Don't ruin this moment for me, Annabelle."

I mouthed the words "I'm sorry" to Lorinda, but she only smiled.

"I feel like he could be a very good customer," she said.

Fern winked at her. "And I feel like you and I are going to become best friends."

I looked past Fern and Kate and the jewelry case as a collective wave of whispers passed through the room. A tall broad-shouldered man had walked in, and it seemed like every woman had sensed his presence and now stared in his direction. He had wavy brown hair that curled around the nape of his neck and dark eyes that, even from where I stood, drew me in with their intensity.

This man belonged on a movie set, not at a bridal show. For a moment I wondered if he was a groom trying to sneak in early before I saw a hairbrush in his hand and a model with her hair done up in a jet-black beehive standing next to him. If this was Christopher I could understand why Fern hated him. He was stunning. I almost hated him and I was a woman.

"Is that Christopher?" I asked.

Fern followed my gaze and sucked in air. "What is he doing down here?"

"That's the other hairdresser?" Kate's face registered surprise, then admiration. The only thing that could pry her away from a case filled with diamonds was a man as beautiful as Christopher.

"You didn't tell us that the models were wearing beehives," I said. "How retro."

"Don't look at me." Fern made a face of disgust as he ran his eyes over the bouffant hairdo. "That's all Christopher. I wanted to do beachy waves."

"You've been known to do big hair before," Kate said.

Fern held up a finger. "There's big and then there's hive. I only do hive if I've had too many cocktails."

Christopher and his model walked to the far side of the room, and then our line of vision became blocked by the drape walls. Kate craned her neck until she stumbled a few feet.

Fern sniffed. "The worst part? He's actually a ladies' man. I can't compete with that."

"Really?" Kate smoothed her hair as her eyes scanned the room, presumably to find out where the hunky hairdresser had gone.

"Why do you think he's getting his way with all the women who run this show?" Fern threw back his shoulders and fluffed his colorful ascot with both hands. "But if that's the way it's going to be around here, maybe I'll leave. They won't have Fern to push around any longer."

He strode out of the ballroom, one hand on his hip, without a backward glance.

"Is your friend always so dramatic?" Lorinda asked.

"Yes," I said. "Always."

"Do you think he'll bring back my ring?" she asked.

Great. Fern had been wearing her three-carat cushion cut when he flounced out. "I'll get it back for you."

"I'll come," Kate said. "It may take both of us to pry it off his finger."

We'd only made it a few feet away from the jewelry display when the lights in the ballroom went out and the entire room was engulfed in darkness.

Strike one for the bridal show.

CHAPTER 3

A few screams then low murmuring followed the plunge into darkness.

I reached out for Kate and grabbed her arm. She yelped and tried to pull her arm away.

"It's just me," I told her.

Her arm relaxed. "Warn me next time you grab me in the dark."

"Who else would it be?" I asked. "I'm the only person standing next to you."

"I don't know," she said. "What do we do now?"

My eyes searched in the dark for the emergency exit signs, but since we were in the middle of the room with fabric walls down the sides, we couldn't see any doors. Even the main doors were blocked by fabric that was still being hung.

So this was why the fire marshal had a fit about us blocking exit signs with décor, I thought.

"Do you think the whole hotel lost power or did we blow out a fuse down here?" Kate asked, now clutching onto my arm.

"No clue." Chances were good that the musicians, caterers, lighting crew, and sound engineers had plugged in enough equipment to short out the city not to mention a renovated hundred-year-old hotel.

I could hear people fumbling and bumping around and a few yells on the other side of the room about a fuse box. The closest person to us was the jeweler, but she hadn't made any noise since the lights had gone out. "Lorinda?"

"I'm over here." Her voice came from where I guessed the jewelry case stood a few feet away from me. "Hey!" she yelped, and I heard a thump followed by some clattering and scuffling.

"Are you okay?" Kate asked.

"Someone knocked me over," Lorinda said.

Who was walking around pushing people in the dark? "Hold on. We're coming." I shuffled my way toward her voice in the dark, pulling Kate along with me. "Where are you?"

"Here, but I'm already up."

I groped a few feet in front of me and found her arm. The lights came on, and I blinked at the brightness. Kate, Lorinda, and I stood together in a tight circle holding each other's arms. We all took a step back, then joined the rest of the vendors in the room in clapping.

"Well, that was a little scary," Kate said.

"I'm sure this building wasn't wired to handle an over-the-top bridal show," I said. "At least they came back on."

"Can you believe that?" Buster walked up and dropped an armload of leafy gold branches next to us, making the pile nearly waist high. His partner, Mack, came behind him with a tall gilded vase filled with a cascade of white orchids.

Mack placed the arrangement on our gold bar. "We were in the hallway from the loading dock when the power went out, if you can imagine that."

Buster, the taller and wider of the two floral designers, adjusted the motorcycle goggles on top of his bald head and brushed some flower pollen off his black leather vest. "It was terrifying. We only had the exit sign for light. Not that I could see over those branches anyway."

Mack came up and gave me a quick kiss on the cheek, his goatee tickling me and the chains on his leather motorcycle pants jingling as he moved. Aside from owning one of the city's top floral-design shops, Buster and Mack belonged to a Christian motorcycle gang. This meant they rode top of the line Harley-Davidson bikes, wore lots of black leather, and did not approve of swearing.

"At least you didn't drop the flowers." Kate motioned to the arrangement they'd made for us.

Mack's sucked in air. "Of course not. Do you know the street value of all these phalaenopsis orchids?"

"I can't thank you enough for doing our space for us," I said. Lush was providing all of our flowers for the show as well as the gold branches that would hang over our two spaces.

Buster waved off my thanks. "We're happy to do it. As long as you keep bringing us more brides wearing huge rocks."

"That reminds me." I turned to Lorinda, who still stood next to her glass case. "This is Lorinda Goodman from Goodman & Sons Jewelers."

Buster and Mack both stepped over to shake her hand, but Lorinda stood staring down at her case without looking up.

"Lorinda?" I said. "Are you okay?"

When she raised her head, her eyes were wide, and her mouth hung open. I wondered if maybe she'd hit her head when she'd fallen.

"My diamond rings," she said, her voice hollow. "They're gone."

CHAPTER 4

K ate and I rushed over to where Lorinda stood, staring down at her jewelry case. She was right. It was empty. The black velvet trays no longer held rows of glittering rings. The back of the case stood open and the trays were askew, as if they'd been emptied and tossed back in. The business cards on top of the case were scattered and some were wet from where water from the flower vase had spilled out.

"But, how?" Kate asked.

Lorinda rubbed her head, seeming dazed. "Whoever pushed me down must have taken them."

"But wasn't the case locked?" I asked. "I thought you had to open it with a key."

Lorinda shook her head. "I unlocked it to take the ring out for your friend to try on. I didn't close it back before the lights went out."

I glared at Kate who made a point to ignore my gaze. This was all because she and Fern had to try on rings. Then I remembered that Fern still had one of Lorinda's rings. Maybe the only ring that hadn't been stolen.

"Should we call hotel security?" Buster asked.

I nodded. "The thief couldn't have gotten far. If we can have the hotel lock this place down, maybe there's a chance of finding them."

Buster hurried off while Mack came over and put an arm around Lorinda. "Why don't you sit down?" He led her to one of our bar stools.

"This has never happened to me before." She perched on the edge of the stool, her shoulders slumped. "And I know it never happened to my father. What is he going to say when he finds out?"

"Maybe he doesn't have to find out." Kate slid onto the stool next to Lorinda.

"I don't think I can hide the fact that I lost a quarter of a million dollars in diamond rings."

Mack mouthed over Lorinda's bent head, "A quarter of a million dollars?"

"I know," I mouthed back. I couldn't imagine walking around with that much worth of anything. I could only hope she had good insurance.

"I think what Kate means is that he won't need to hear about it if the diamonds can be recovered." I glanced at my assistant. "Right?"

"Exactly," Kate said. "Solving crimes is kind of a hobby of ours."

"Well," I started to correct Kate. I didn't want anyone to think that we enjoyed getting caught up in criminal cases. It was purely bad luck that had caused us to be involved in the past. I didn't need to get involved anymore. Weddings were challenging enough without throwing murder and theft into the mix.

Lorinda sat up. "So you could get my diamonds back?"

I gave Kate a pointed look that said I would kill her later for offering us up as makeshift detectives. "We might have been involved in a few cases . . ."

"You have to help me." Lorinda clutched my hands. "If my

father finds out that inventory was stolen under my watch, I don't know what he'll do. He still owns the company, and he's not very pleased with me right now as it is. Sales are down. That's why I'm doing the show. I have to get the business back in the black and prove to him that I can run the store as well as any son would."

No one spoke for a moment, and I wondered if Lorinda regretted confessing so much to people she barely knew.

Buster ran back up, breathing heavily. "Okay, the hotel is locked down, and security is right behind me."

"Security will know what to do," I told Lorinda as I spotted two tall men approaching us in black suits and carrying hand-held radios.

As long as we didn't have to involve the police. I did not want my name mentioned alongside another crime. With my bad luck, Detective Reese would hear about it and show up. I wasn't sure if I was up to seeing him again. Things with the handsome detective were always too confusing.

CHAPTER 5

"**S**o tell me what happened when the lights went out," the taller and darker of the two security guards asked Lorinda. His partner, who had hair so pale I wondered if he was part albino, inspected the jewelry case without touching it while we sat on bar stools at the gold bar. Mack and Buster had returned to designing their space while we were being questioned.

Lorinda took a shaky breath. "I was behind the case when everything went black. Annabelle and her assistant were on the other side a few feet away. Then I got pushed to the ground, and I heard some noises. That must have been when they took the rings. Then the person must have run off because by the time I stood up and felt around, no one was there."

The guard questioning us looked to Kate and me. "Is this what you heard, too?"

"It all happened pretty fast, but I definitely heard some scuffling and clattering, which I now know must have been someone messing with the case," I said.

"There was a lot of bumping around all over the room. It was hard to know what was going on or where the noises came from," Kate added. "But I heard noises near the jewelry case, too."

"And your case was unlocked?" The other security officer called from where he hunched over the jewelry case.

Lorinda flushed. "I'd opened it to show a ring and hadn't closed it again before the lights went off."

"So anyone could have taken the rings," the pale guard said, more of a statement than a question.

"I suppose so," Lorinda admitted. "The sliding door to the back of the case was wide open."

"But you could only see that if you were standing close enough," Kate said.

The guard doing the questioning nodded. "And how many people were close enough to see that?"

Kate glanced around her. "Fern had walked off, Buster and Mack were still in the back, and Richard had returned to his booth. So at that point it would have been the three of us."

I glared at her. She'd just implicated us as possible suspects in the burglary. She cringed as she realized what she'd done.

"But we don't have any motive to steal the rings." Kate jerked her head in my direction. "Annabelle barely wears jewelry and can't accessorize to save her life."

"Thanks, Kate," I said. "Very helpful."

"Do you mind if we search your bags?" The pale security officer joined us.

"Be my guest." I waved toward the canvas bags sitting on the floor.

Kate walked behind the bar and handed over her black Longchamp bag. "Knock yourselves out."

"What's going on?" Richard asked as he walked up.

"Lorinda's diamond rings were stolen when the lights went out," Kate said, coming out from behind the bar.

Richard's eyes widened. "What? Who?"

"Richard, this is Lorinda Goodman of Goodman & Sons Jewelers." I touched Lorinda's shoulder. "Lorinda, this is Richard Gerard. He's a caterer."

Richard gave me a cutting glance, which told me I'd given him too perfunctory an introduction. "We've actually met before."

She shook his hand, her face puzzled.

"I catered your father's retirement party two years ago," Richard said. "You probably don't remember."

"I'm sorry. I wasn't very involved in planning the party. My mother handled that," Lorinda said. "But I'm surprised you remember a small party from over a year ago."

Richard seemed pleased with himself. "I never forget a client's name or face. Considering some of my clients, it's both a blessing and a curse."

"All right, ladies." The taller security guard passed Kate her bag. "We've searched all your bags and didn't find anything."

Richard raised an eyebrow. "They think you took the rings?"

I shrugged. "We were closest to the case when the lights went off."

"I mean maybe Kate," Richard said. "But you've never known how to wear jewelry, Annabelle."

Kate grinned. "That's what I told them."

I folded my arms over my chest. "Very funny, you two."

"We're going to search all the booths and bags in case the thief is still in the ballroom," the other security guard said. "And no one is stepping foot out of the hotel without being searched."

"What about the show?" Mack asked. He'd sidled over from the Lush display, where Buster stood on a ladder attaching branches to a metal arch.

One of the guards glanced at his watch. "It doesn't start for another three hours. That should give us enough time to do a thorough search."

"So there's no chance you'll cancel it, is there?" Mack asked, his eyes darting to the piles of gilded branches being suspended over-head and the massive orchid cascade on the bar. I knew he was mentally calculating how much money they'd lose if the show was rescheduled and they had to order all new flowers.

"I can't make any promises," the blond guard told him. "Once three hundred brides come in here, the chance of finding those rings goes right out the window."

Lorinda put her elbows on the bar and let her head drop. "My father is going to fire me for sure."

"Don't worry." Kate rubbed her back. "I'm sure we'll find them."

"Please don't call the police yet," Lorinda said to the security guards. "I don't want to have to file a report if I don't have to."

The guards both eyed her. "Why not?"

She lowered her eyes. "My father. I'd rather he not find out unless he absolutely must."

"It's our policy to call the police for something of this magnitude," the dark-haired guard said. "But we can postpone calling them until after we've made our preliminary search and investigation."

Lorinda beamed at him. "Thank you."

"But that won't take long so if you don't want to file a police report or have the show canceled, you'd better hope those rings turn up sooner rather than later."

With that, the security guards walked away from us and started talking to the photographers who were two booths down.

Mack's face fell and a branch crashed to the floor behind us. We looked over to where Buster stood on the ladder.

"Canceled?" Buster looked like he'd been punched in the gut. "Impossible. Not after all the work we've done, all the money we've put into this."

"I have several hundred profiteroles in spun sugar cages," Richard said, his face turning pink. "And don't get me started on the brownie meringue pops that took me forever to arrange standing up in a bed of colored sugar."

Mack hurried over to the base of Buster's ladder and retrieved the fallen branch. "That's only a worst-case scenario. That's not going to happen, right?" He stared at me, his face begging me to back him up.

"If it does, the hotel is getting a bill from me." Richard stomped off.

I thought of the two options. Option one: the police. The thought of filing a police report clearly upset Lorinda. If her father was as tough on her as it sounded, I understood her wanting to hide a mistake like leaving the jewelry case open and getting robbed.

Option two: canceling the show. Even if they could find another weekend where all the vendors were free before wedding season picked up, Buster and Mack couldn't afford to buy all the flowers again and Richard would bust a gasket if he had to throw away all of the food he'd prepared. No. The show must go on.

"Of course it's not going to be canceled," I said. "Because we're going to find out who took those diamonds."

CHAPTER 6

"**D**on't we need to set up our display?" Kate asked as I pulled her by the sleeve toward the middle of the room.

"We can't do much until Buster and Mack hang the canopy of branches," I said. "Unless you want to find us helmets to wear as we work underneath them."

Kate shook her head, no doubt thinking back to the large branch that had crashed to the floor under Buster only minutes ago.

The setup of the show had resumed after the blackout, and the ballroom bustled with activity. The makeup artist across from us had suspended an ornate silver-framed mirror in front of her stool and bent over a long narrow table arranging the rows of brushes, shadows, blushes, and pencils she would use on the brides-to-be. She wore her black hair naturally curly and short and always rocked a perfect winged cat eye.

"Let me know if you ladies want a touch-up before the show," she called to us.

I felt Kate start to drift in the direction of the MAC and Bobbi Brown logos, and I tightened my grip on her arm. Since the makeup artist hadn't been at her booth during the blackout, she didn't make my list of people to interview. "Later, I promise."

Next to the makeup artist, stood a space designed entirely in shades of blue from the turquoise backdrop to the navy-blue linen covering a long rectangular table to the thick garland of indigo flowers running the length of the table and touching the floor on either side.

"Are those spray painted?" I whispered to Kate. Not a huge number of flowers found in nature actually came in blue, and I felt reasonably confident that carnations were not one of them.

Kate grimaced. "A better question is are those carnations?"

"Carnations in mass can be pretty," I said.

"Then this needs more mass."

I elbowed her in the side as the florist turned from putting the finishing touches on her spray-painted carnation runner. I glanced up at the sign over the table: Tamara's Flowers. "You must be Tamara."

The woman smiled and pushed a strand of brown hair out of her face. She dropped a pair of clippers into the front pouch of her Tamara's Flowers apron. "Tammy Roland. Nice to meet you."

"I'm Annabelle and this is my assistant, Kate." I shook her hand, then Kate did the same. "It seems like the blackout didn't slow you down much."

Tammy laughed. "Nah. I came in here real early setting up. It's my first show, and I wanted to get it just right. Have you two done this show before?"

"I few times," I said. "It's the best one."

"Is it always in this hotel?" Tammy asked.

"No, it moves around," Kate said. "But this is the first year we've lost power during setup."

"Wasn't that something?" Tammy shook her head. "I was unpacking my garland when it went black."

"So you were behind the table?" I asked.

"Nope. Right in front of it." She motioned to some empty boxes near us. "I had my boxes outside of my space a bit."

I glanced at the long white flower boxes jutting out into the center of the room. "So did you hear anyone moving around or running past you during the blackout?"

Tammy tilted her head to one side. "Running past me? No. But there were definitely folks moving around and bumping into things. I almost fell over trying to find my table."

"I'll bet." I thought back to when Kate and I groped our way over to Lorinda in the dark. It made sense that we weren't the only people trying to move around the room.

"Are you asking because of the lady who got her diamonds stolen?"

I must have appeared surprised because Tammy grinned and rested her fingers on my arm. "It's not a huge room, and eavesdropping is one of my hobbies."

I couldn't help liking Tammy. "Well, if you hear anything that might help us find out who took the diamonds, we're right over in the booth with the gold bar."

Tammy's eyes darted over my shoulders to where our gold bar sat underneath an ever-growing canopy of gold branches. Mack stood on the ground directly underneath Buster and passed up another branch. "You know the boys from Lush?"

"Buster and Mack?" Kate said. "Sure."

Tammy's cheeks flushed. "Would you mind introducing me? Whenever you get the chance or even after the show."

"Of course," I said. "Stop by after all the brides leave, and we'll introduce you."

We left Tammy excited for her meeting with Buster and Mack, but we hadn't gained much new information.

"What the . . ." Kate stopped short in front of the next booth and I bumped into her back.

I stepped around Kate to see what had caught her attention. A pink sign for Brianna's Bride's Wedding Planning hung over an all-white display. A deathly white woman in a white lab coat stood between a Plexiglas swivel stool and a narrow table that held a row of syringes. "Is that what I think it is?"

"Botox," Kate whispered to me. "This wedding planner is giving out free Botox injections."

"That can't be legal," I said, imagining the fits my insurance company would have if I told them I'd be performing medical procedures.

Kate dug an elbow into my side and motioned to the sign on an easel next to the woman. *Erase your worry and your worry lines by becoming one of Brianna's Brides today!* The words were emblazoned in hot pink and surrounded by pictures of hearts and wedding rings.

Kate shook her head slowly. "We can't compete with this."

"Are you kidding me?" I asked. "What kind of crazy person would want to be injected with a toxin at a bridal fair?" I held up a finger "Aside from you."

"Brides," Kate reminded me. "They're exactly this kind of crazy."

"Who is this Brianna anyway? Have you ever heard of her?"

"Never," Kate said. "Do you think she's the one in the lab coat?"

"No." I jerked my head toward a tall blonde who'd appeared from behind the drape in the back of the booth. She wore a fuchsia cocktail dress and sparkly silver shoes that seemed out of place next to a woman in a lab coat. Or at a bridal show.

She spotted us and beamed. "Hey, y'all."

"Hi," I said. "I'm Annabelle and this is Kate. We're from Wedding Belles."

She nodded but didn't register any recognition. "I've never heard of your company. Are you new, too?"

Kate made a noise of indignant protest, but I talked over her. "We've been around for about five years."

"Really? Well, I'm Brianna. I recently moved up from Charleston."

"So you're doing Botox today?" Kate asked.

Brianna leaned in to us. "Isn't this fun? One of the first things I noticed about DC was how serious it is." She made an exaggerated pouty face. "And so many girls have worry lines already. This is just me doing my part to make Washington pretty again."

Kate and I stared at her.

"Y'all are more than welcome to get your foreheads done before the brides get here."

"That's so sweet of you," I said before Kate could come back with what was sure to be a tart reply. "We're actually asking around to see if anyone heard a person running out of the ballroom during the blackout."

Brianna's eyes widened but her eyebrows didn't move. I suspected she'd already sampled her own wares. "How mysterious. Now that you mention it, I do remember hearing someone pass by me awfully fast."

"During the blackout?" I asked.

"Mmm-hmm. Maybe a minute or so after everything went black."

I made a mental note that Brianna's Botox display stood only one booth away from the door to the ballroom.

"Thanks," I said. "That's very helpful."

"Y'all don't forget to come back here for your Botox," she said as I moved Kate away from her. "I promise it will take ten years off your face."

"Ten years?" Kate hissed as I propelled her out of earshot. "How old does she think we are?"

"I'm sure she meant to be nice," I said.

Kate rolled her eyes. "I'm sure she didn't. And what about that line that she'd never heard of us? We're in every magazine and on every vendor list in the city."

"That's assuming she reads."

Kate allowed herself a smile. "Touché, Annabelle. I love it when you're snarky."

We'd reached the propped-open double doors to the ballroom. I spotted the two security officers we'd met earlier coming across the foyer toward us, propelling a struggling man between them.

"I'm telling you, this is all a misunderstanding."

Kate turned around when she heard the voice. "Well, we've found Fern."

CHAPTER 7

"I promise you, I did not steal this ring," Fern protested as he entered the ballroom with a security guard on each side. "I was merely making a dramatic statement."

"That's true," I said, walking up to the two security officers. "He was trying on the ring right before the blackout."

Neither officer seemed convinced. "Then why did we find him getting on an elevator?"

"He was in the middle of flouncing out of the ballroom in protest when the power went out," Kate said.

The taller officer loosened his grip as he gave Fern the once-over. "Protesting what?"

"The indignity of having to work with a marginally talented stylist." Fern's voice cracked as he let his head flop forward. "The horror of being eclipsed before my star has been allowed to fully shine."

"Okay." The blond officer shook his head. "How about I take the ring and return it to the jeweler for you?"

Fern snapped his head back up. "That works for me." He slid the diamond ring off his finger and dropped it into one of the officer's opened palm. The two men released his arms and Fern smoothed his velvet smoking jacket. "I hope these creases in the velvet aren't permanent."

"Looks like you're having a bit of trouble, buddy." Christopher clapped a hand on Fern's shoulder as he came around the drape wall.

Fern stumbled forward a step then righted himself. "No. A little misunderstanding is all."

Kate rested a hand on my arm to steady herself as she took in Christopher at close range. I stared pointedly at Kate, hoping she'd get my message to take her gaping down a notch. Either she didn't notice the message or pretended not to. "I'm Kate. A friend of Fern's."

Christopher gave her a spectacular smile. "Any friend of Fern's is a friend of mine."

I had to admit that not only was this guy gorgeous, he seemed charming. I could tell why Fern despised him. If I met a female equivalent, I'd want to pull out her hair.

Fern had a forced smile on his face, but I could practically hear him seething inside. "What are you doing down here, Christopher?"

"Taking a peek at the ballroom before it all starts." He swept his arms wide. "But I was headed back up. Don't want to fall behind in glamming up these models, do we?" He placed a hand on the back of the model standing next to him, a picture in her beehive, nearly sheer wedding gown, and matching elbow-length sheer gloves. The dark-haired waif made quite the contrast to his bulk. Her bored gaze passed over us, but she didn't spare even the hint of a smile.

"If the show isn't shut down," I said.

"Why?" Fern and Christopher asked simultaneously.

I pointed to Fern's now-bare finger. "The ring you had on your finger wasn't the only one that walked off. Goodman & Sons Jewelers was robbed."

Fern gasped. "During the blackout?"

Kate nodded. "Someone got all of her diamond rings."

Fern staggered into Kate, who nearly buckled under his weight. "All those diamonds are gone?"

I ignored Fern's mock swoon and turned to Christopher. "You were here when the lights went out, right?"

He motioned to the right side of the drape wall. "I wanted to inspect my booth before the fashion show started. You know we're given a free booth for doing the hair for the show?"

I glanced at Fern, who gave a small nod and said under his breath, "I asked to be on the opposite side."

"I'm next to the bespoke tuxedo booth all the way at the end." Christopher grinned. "They're interested in having me model for them."

"I'll bet they are," Kate said. This time Fern stepped on her foot, causing her to yelp and glare at him. At this rate, they would be in a full-on brawl within five minutes.

"Did you see anything?" I asked Christopher, doing my best not to pay any attention to Kate and Fern.

"Well it was pitch dark," Christopher said and laughed at his own wit.

"Hear anything then?" I corrected myself. "Or notice anyone running around?"

Christopher cocked his head at me. "In the dark? No. I mean, people were talking and trying to find their way to an exit but no one was crazy enough to run around. The floor is still covered with boxes. They'd break their neck."

He made a good point. The ballroom remained pretty chaotic and messy. It would be difficult to take a step without having to dodge a crate or a pile of branches or a rack of glassware.

"What about when the lights came back on?" I asked.

He smiled at the model next to him. "I spent a few minutes talking to the tuxedo guys, and now I'm here talking to you."

"Right," I said. "I'm only asking to help find the missing rings.

If they have to call in the police, that could mean the end of the bridal show."

Christopher's face fell. "But we've been working on these models since eight a.m."

"We've all been here for a while," Kate said. "That's why we're asking around. We find the diamonds, the show goes on."

"Well, you know where I was," Fern said.

"Had you made it to the elevators when the lights went out?" I asked.

Fern tapped a finger to his chin. "No. I was on the stairs from the foyer to the elevator bank. When everything went black, I froze."

"Who else was in the foyer and stairs with you?"

"Lots of people." He shuddered. "The poor lighting team still on ladders."

"Did you hear anyone running past you for the exit?"

Fern pursed his mouth while he thought. "Running? I don't think so. But someone could have walked past me. There was a lot of noise with the guys trying to come down from the ladders. One of them slipped and yelled pretty loud."

"Well, we'd better head back upstairs. We have a dress rehearsal for the show in a few minutes." Christopher thumped Fern on the back as he moved toward the door, guiding the model with a hand resting on the small of her back. A security guard stopped the pair, giving Christopher a pat-down, then seeing the tiny girl in the form-fitting gossamer gown and waving her through. There wasn't room between her skin and the fabric for a tissue much less a tray of diamond rings.

"Can you believe him?" Fern hissed once Christopher walked out of earshot.

"No." Kate stared after him. "He's almost too good to be true."

Fern glared at Kate. "So this is what betrayal feels like."

Kate slipped an arm around Fern's waist. "You know I love you the most."

He sniffed. "Talk is cheap, darling. But I suppose the beefcake is right. I'd better go back upstairs. You'll come see our dress rehearsal, won't you?"

"When is it? We still need to talk to a lot of people down here about the theft." I spotted the security officers walking toward us and tried to change the subject. "But text me before it starts, and we'll come upstairs."

"If we can," Kate said. "This crime isn't going to investigate itself."

I stared at her, willing her to be quiet, but as usual, she missed my signal. How could she pick up a single guy's signals from miles away yet miss all of mine?

"Very funny." I gave Kate a playful shove as the security officers got within earshot. "You're such a kidder."

"I wish it was a joke," Kate said. "You know that there are few things Annabelle loves as much as poking her nose into a crime when she's told not to."

"Is that so?" The stern expression on the tall officer's face told me that he wasn't amused.

CHAPTER 8

"**D**o we have a problem here?" The security officer folded his thick arms across his chest.

Kate and Fern had been struck dumb once they'd realized that the head of security had walked up behind them. Fern's eyes had bugged out to fish-like proportions while Kate's mouth hung open.

"No problem," I said. "We were only joking."

He didn't appear convinced. "It sounded like this isn't the first crime you've been involved in."

"What? No, I mean, like we mentioned earlier, we've been involved in one or two incidents before," I said.

"One or two?" His gaze narrowed.

"Or three," I added.

He snapped his fingers. "Wait a second. Did you have anything to do with the murder at the Fairmont Hotel?"

"The Mayflower Hotel was the last one, actually," Kate said. "The Fairmont was the time before."

Now it was the officer's turn to appear surprised.

I glared at Kate. "You're not helping."

"He should be glad to have wedding planners like us around,"

Kate said. "We always helped the DC police solve the cases. Mostly by almost getting killed but, still, it was a help."

"Sometimes I got to wear a costume," Fern said. "I make a very convincing priest."

Both officers shifted their eyes from Fern to Kate and then to me. The darker one cleared his throat. "Let me be very clear. I do not need wedding planners running their own investigation. I do not want wedding planners running their own investigation. I do not want anyone wearing a costume."

Fern dismissed him with a glance. "Your loss. My performance was Oscar-worthy."

The blond officer leveled a finger at all three of us. "No investigating. I have this completely under control."

"Fine," I said. "We were only trying to help by asking people if they noticed anyone running—"

The darker officer cut me off. "Let us do the questioning, okay?"

I nodded but didn't respond.

He took a deep breath. "We called this in to the police—"

"What?" I cried. "But you promised Lorinda you'd wait."

The officer leveled his eyes at me. "If you'd let me continue, I was going to say that they can't send a team right away. Some sort of incident across town has most of their officers tied up so they won't be here right away."

I sighed with relief. There was a still a chance to save Lorinda's skin and keep the show on schedule.

"But my team is combing every inch of the building until the police arrive." He paused. "And we're questioning everyone."

"I'm glad to hear it," I said.

Fern cleared his throat. "If that's all, I need to go upstairs to finish the models for the fashion show."

"You'll have to be patted down by my guys if you leave the ballroom," the paler of the two officers said.

Fern eyed the two burly men posted at the doors. "Don't mind if I do." He winked at Kate and me over his shoulder as he headed toward the doors.

Once the security duo had walked off, Kate let out a breath. "What a killjoy. He's not nearly as fun as Detective Reese."

"No, he's not," I agreed. Detective Reese would have warned us off, as well, but he would have done it with a flirtatious smile. "And I doubt he has as much experience catching real criminals."

"As a hotel security guard? Doubtful," Kate said. "The only hotels that have had serious crimes are the ones we've done weddings in."

I cringed at the truth of that statement. "Thanks for reminding me that we're the wedding planner angels of death."

"No one calls us that," Kate said. "Well, maybe Richard. But he's one to talk."

"Do you really think this hotel security team has any chance of catching a jewel thief who seems to have planned out their crime pretty well?" I started walking down the side of the room and Kate followed me. We passed a DJ in a tuxedo setting up. his laptop. Gone were the days of turntables or boxes filled with CDs. All a DJ needed these days was a laptop, a digital library of music, and a pair of speakers.

"Not really. But you heard what he said. We can't be involved in this." Kate paused at an unmanned booth displaying bridal veils and put a lace mantilla on her head.

I shook my head. "Too virginal for you. Even if we can't investigate, they can't stop us from putting together what we know so far."

Kate replaced the veil on the mannequin head. "Which is?"

"When the lights went out, someone made their way to the jewelry case, pushed Lorinda down, took the rings out of the open case, and hurried out of the ballroom." I continued down the colonnade of wedding booths until I reached the one for Richard Gerard Catering.

"We think they left the ballroom," Kate corrected me. "They

37

could have stashed them somewhere in the room to retrieve later. The lights weren't off for very long."

Richard came around to join us from behind his tiered food display. Frosted glass shelving filled with confections covered the back of his space. Tarts, brownies, cookies, towers of profiteroles. The table in front held small bowls and tiny plates of shrimp and grits, shredded duck tacos, and vegetarian beggar's purses all displayed on Plexiglas cubes with the name of the food written in lavender calligraphy.

"The lights were off long enough, thank you very much," Richard said. "I was terrified that people were going to start running and knock over my glass shelving."

Kate glanced at Richard, then his food display, then him again. "Did you match the calligraphy on the Plexi food stands to your shirt?"

"Well done." He smoothed the front of his lavender button-down. "I hoped one of you would notice."

"Sorry," I said. "My mind is on this robbery."

"Any luck so far?" Richard asked.

"I can't figure out how someone could cut the power and make their way around the room to the jewelry case before the lights came back on," I said. "The Goodman & Sons booth is in the middle of the room."

"Well, one of the lighting panels is right there." Richard pointed to a panel on the wall across from him covered in the same fabric as the hotel walls.

"Did the security team check it for prints?" I asked.

Richard put a hand on his hip. "This is not *CSI*. That thing is covered with prints. Everyone who works in this hotel uses it to adjust the lights not to mention the lighting crew for the show. I doubt they'll find anything useful."

"Good point," I said. "But even if someone killed the lights from here, they didn't have time to walk all the way around the room."

"You're forgetting the possibility that two people pulled off the heist," Richard said. "One to cut the lights and the other to snatch the diamonds."

"So the person who took the diamonds could have been near us when the lights went off. The fastest way would have been to go past Buster and Mack's booth, snatch the rings, then leave the same way," Kate said.

"Except that Brianna said she heard someone run past her," I reminded her.

Kate wrinkled her nose. "Right. I forgot about Botox Barbie."

"So who has the booths closest to the end of the room?" I walked beyond the Richard Gerard Catering space. "There are only a few more down here."

We passed the cosmetic dentistry display, which was devoid of dentists for the moment.

Richard giggled. "I think my sugar is getting to them. They've gone through so much sugarless gum that I'm afraid lockjaw will set in before the show starts. I think they finally had to step outside."

Next to the dentists stood Christopher's booth, near the end of the row. Instead of the ivory drape that everyone else used, he'd draped his space in crushed red velvet. A black velvet tufted stool sat in the center of the space, and an ornate gold mirror hung in front of it with the words "Hair by Christopher" written in a flowery script around the top of the glass.

Kate took a step back. "Wow."

"It's like Vampira meets Versailles," Richard said.

"The questionable choice of beehives is starting to make more sense." I peered around to see if any of the security team was nearby. "Let's see if there's anything suspicious about our hunky hairstylist."

I lifted the edge of one of the black velvet cloths covering his table. Nothing underneath save an empty crate. And nothing on top of the table except for bottles of hairspray and clear glass jars of brushes and bobby pins. "Nothing. Not that I expected to find anything."

"Well, this may be something," Kate said.

I straightened up and focused on Kate holding back a panel of red velvet drape. Christopher's booth backed right up to Buster and Mack's booth on the other side of the fabric wall.

"All you would have to do is pull back this material and voila," Kate said. "You'd be on the other side and only a few steps away from the Goodman & Sons display."

Now things were getting interesting.

CHAPTER 9

"**S**o he had easy access to the other side," I said after Kate had dropped the drape. "But what's his motive?"

"Lots of pretty diamonds?"

I gazed around me at the gaudy but sparse space. "Okay, I'll go with your theory that the cute but dumb hairdresser managed to cut the power, pass through the drape to our side, and snatch the diamonds. But then where did he put them? We saw him get patted down when he left the room."

"Don't forget that his accomplice could have cut the power," Richard said. "Giving him more time to grab and then stash the rings."

"What accomplice?" I pulled my phone out of my jeans as it pinged to let me know I had a text.

"He's a hairdresser," Richard said. "What about the model?"

"That waif in the too-tight, see-through dress? She can barely move in that thing, so I doubt she'd be much help. Besides, she's a model the show provided. I doubt he's laid eyes on her before today." I read the text from Fern. "The dress rehearsal for the fashion show is about to begin."

Richard's face perked up. "I'm up for a fashion show. Anything to save me from the DJ's sound checks."

"Well, you're wrong there," Kate said.

I held out my phone. "I don't think so. He says to come up ASAP."

"No, about Christopher and the model. He's definitely dating her."

"How can you know something like that?" I asked Kate as we walked with Richard toward the ballroom exit. We paused to be cleared by the security team that was frisking everyone leaving the ballroom with Richard complaining loudly that they were wrinkling his shirt.

"The real question is when have you ever known me to be wrong about something that involves dating?" Kate asked.

"You make a good point." Kate did boast an uncanny ability to determine if a couple was involved and even *how* involved with a single glance. She considered it her superpower.

"And you know that Christopher is dating the model because . . ?"

Kate reached over and rested her hand on the small of Richard's back.

He took a step away. "I beg your pardon?"

"Exactly." She snapped her fingers. "That's not something you do to a colleague or a friend or a model you just met this morning. But Christopher did that to this model, and that tells me that he knows her. Very well."

I nodded at Kate in admiration. "You're like Sherlock Holmes meets Tinder."

"Look at you talking about Tinder," she said. "I'm swelling with pride."

"Just because I've heard about swiping right on your phone to meet Mr. Right doesn't meet I have any intention to ever use the app." The thought of dating being distilled down to an app on my smartphone that offered me pictures of men to either accept (swipe right) or reject (swipe left) horrified me. I'd convinced myself that I'd rather stay single than resort to finger swiping.

"Too bad," Kate said. "I'd be happy to help you swipe."

I pushed the call button for the elevators. "That's what I'm afraid of."

"Richard, tell Annabelle that she's being ridiculous about dating apps."

"Annabelle, you're being ridiculous if you're using dating apps," he said.

"That's not what I meant, and you know it." Kate swatted at him as the far elevator doors pinged and then opened.

Richard held his palm against the motion sensitive elevator doors as Kate and I stepped on. The elevator closed, and I pushed the button for the top floor.

"Remind me again why you care so much about these diamonds?" Richard asked as the elevator surged upward.

I forgot that he'd stomped off before I'd promised Lorinda that we would find out who'd taken her diamonds. "So Lorinda can recover her diamonds and the show won't be canceled."

Richard crossed his arms over his chest. "And why, pray tell, are the police not involved? Wouldn't things go faster if there were detectives here?"

"The police are busy with something else," I said. "Plus, Lorinda doesn't want to file a police report if she can avoid it. She says her father will crucify her if he finds out."

Richard nodded. "Well, she's right about her father. He's awful, and he'd most certainly blame her."

"You seem to know a lot about the man," Kate said.

"I only met him once, but he falls into my top ten list of unpleasant clients," Richard said.

"Wow, that's saying something." I'd worked with enough of Richard's clients to know that those were bold words.

Richard studied me. "So you're determined to find the

diamonds before the police arrive because you and Lorinda are such good friends?"

"Not entirely," I said, stepping out of the elevator the second it arrived at the top floor of the hotel. "I do want to help her. I feel bad for her as another businesswoman who's working hard to get ahead. I also don't want to police to shut down the show."

"Are those the only reasons?" Kate asked.

Richard chased after me as I strode down the hallway to the right. "Are they?"

I stopped in front of the large white doors leading to the Altitude Ballroom. "There may be a small part of me that isn't eager to run into Detective Reese."

Richard darted a hand out and held it against the doors so I couldn't open them. "You know he isn't the only officer on the force. The chances he'd show up to a burglary are small."

"Not with my luck," I muttered.

"Anyway, how hard could it be to find a few diamonds?" Kate asked. She pulled open the door to the Altitude Ballroom and we all stared open-mouthed. The ballroom had a wall of windows on the left side with the window shades drawn up to highlight the view and let in light. Funky petal-shaped light fixtures hung from the whitewashed beamed ceiling, and a transparent, illuminated runway extended halfway down the length of the room. Rows of clear Plexiglass chairs surrounded the runway and filled most of the floor space. A white drape embedded with crystals created a backdrop to the runway, and above the runway were thousands of clear wires strung with crystals and suspended so that the room appeared to be dripping in diamonds.

Kate met my eyes. "Well, this could be a problem."

CHAPTER 10

I walked a few steps into the room so that I stood underneath the suspended crystals. I reached up and touched one of the two-inch-long clear crystals dangling overhead. A hole had been drilled into the top so it could be strung. "No one would mistake these for a diamond."

"Not when you get up close," Kate agreed with me.

Richard stood next to me, his head tilted back. "And I seriously doubt the thief would have had to time to transport the rings out of the downstairs ballroom and up to the top floor of the hotel. Much less string the diamonds up over the catwalk."

"If they got the rings out of the ballroom, a smart thief would have walked out of the hotel with them," I said.

"Unless they couldn't." Kate continued walking up to the stage backdrop and fingered one of the gems in the white fabric. "What if their plan was to leave the hotel but they didn't make it and they had to hide the rings somewhere until things cool off?"

Richard cocked an eyebrow at her. "Things cool off?"

"You know," Kate said. "Until the heat is off and they can sneak the diamonds out without security busting them."

Richard motioned his head at Kate. "I hear Godfather but I see Barbie."

Kate stuck her tongue out at him.

The doors on the right side of the room opened and a statuesque woman with a severe blond bun and a clear clipboard stepped in, followed by a row of models in wedding gowns.

"This is a dress rehearsal, ladies," she called as the models walked single file to the back of the stage behind the drape wall. "That means I want you to imagine the room filled with brides."

"Should we leave?" Richard asked.

"You, there." The woman pointed at us. "I need you to be my audience. Sit in the front row."

"I guess not," Kate said.

Richard saluted the woman's back as we scurried to seats facing the runway. We picked up the Tiffany-blue show programs from our chairs and scanned them as the models lined up behind the stage and the lights came on from the corners of the room. I turned around to see a sound and lighting tech standing at a narrow control board in the back right corner.

Kate nudged me. "There's Fern."

I stared up at the stage and could see flashes of his green velvet jacket through the drape. I knew he must have been doing final touch-ups to the models before they hit the runway. Fern always considered himself more than a wedding hairstylist. He helped brides into their gowns, he fluffed their veils, and he calmed their nerves. I often joked that with Fern around, I didn't need to lay eyes on the bride until she was ready to cut the cake.

The music began and the light changed to blue as the first model hit the runway.

"What is that music?" Richard asked.

I cringed. "It sounds like 80s hair-band music played on the violin."

"That's what I thought." Richard nodded. "Interesting choice."

The first model, a blonde in a high beehive, hit the end of the runway and paused so that the A-line skirt of her gown swirled around her legs. She pivoted and, without breaking a smile, tossed two handfuls of iridescent confetti in the air, turned, and walked back down the runway as another model came out. The second model had a smaller beehive and wore a lace fit-and-flare gown.

"Am I losing my mind or are these girls wearing beehives?" Richard said over the strange violin music.

Kate leaned across me to Richard. "Those are two separate questions."

"Charming." He made a face at Kate, then said to me, "I never knew Fern went in for sixies hair."

The second model hit her mark at the end of the runway, threw her confetti and spun around.

The blonde with the clipboard stuck her head through the drape and clapped her hands. "Where is my wind?"

"Wind?" Richard and I mouthed to each other as two fans attached to the ceiling began blowing on the runway.

"Didn't you hear?" I cupped a hand over my mouth and talked into his ear. The music and the fans made it nearly impossible to hear each other. "This wasn't Fern's doing. It was the other hair-dresser's idea."

The lights changed to pink, and the music switched. The next model appeared in a tulle gown with a full skirt and a sheer bolero jacket.

"Is that AC/DC?" Kate mouthed.

The model strode down the runway, flung her confetti over her head and it promptly blew into our faces.

"This is the strangest fashion show I've ever seen," Richard yelled over the fans as he spit confetti out of his mouth. "And I had to sit through a swimwear show at my nana's nursing home once."

Kate poked me in the side as another model emerged from behind the drape wall. "There's the model who's dating Christopher."

"She seems familiar," Richard said.

"She's got an Angelina Jolie thing going on," Kate said. "Without the tattoos and six kids, of course."

As the lights changed to a bright white, the dark-haired girl strutted down the catwalk in the form-fitting organza gown we'd seen downstairs. She was pretty in an unusual way with full lips and wide-set eyes. Kate was spot-on with her comparison to Angelina Jolie. The girl reached the end of the runway and paused.

I grabbed both Kate and Richard's knees on either side of me and squeezed. "Look at her hair."

"I'm looking. It's a beehive. The car crash of hairstyles," Richard said. "I can't pull my eyes away."

"Ouch." Kate rubbed her leg. "What wrong with her . . .?"

Richard sat up, staring at the model more intently. "Wait a second. Is that what I think it is?"

The bright lights were concentrated at the end of the runway, and before the model could toss her confetti in the air, we could see all the diamonds glittering inside her beehive.

CHAPTER 11

"**Y**ou find a security guard, and I'll make sure the model doesn't leave," I yelled in Kate's ear.

"What if it isn't only one model's hair?" Kate yelled back. "What if the diamonds are spread out through all of them?"

I groaned. I hadn't thought of that. Just because we hadn't seen them, it didn't mean they couldn't be tucked away under layers of extensions and hairspray.

"Then I'll make sure none of the girls leave," I called out.

Kate nodded and slipped out of the room as the fashion show continued.

I leaned in close to Richard so he could hear me. "You keep watch on the doors, and I'll go backstage and tell Fern."

I hunched over as I crept down the row of chairs and behind the drape backdrop. I scanned the group of models for Fern. He wasn't hard to spot, as one of the few people not wearing a beehive. I wiggled my way through the models until I reached him.

"We found the missing rings," I said.

"What?" He made hand motions to indicate that he couldn't hear me over the music.

"The rings." I gestured to my ring finger, then pointed to the nearest beehive. "They're in the hair."

Fern squinted at me, then shook his head. I could understand his confusion. The idea sounded ridiculous. But still not as ridiculous as having beehives in a bridal fashion show, if you asked me.

"I'll show you." I tugged him behind me as I made my way through the models to the dark-haired girl coming off the runway. I grabbed her by the arms and reached up for her hair. She pulled away.

"Who are you?" The woman with the clipboard spotted me. "You can't be back here."

"What are you doing?" Fern eyes darted from me to the woman.

I made another grab for the beehive. "Help me reach in her hair."

The woman with the clipboard closed the few feet between us and swatted at me with her clipboard, connecting with my knuckles. I jerked my hand back and yelped. The model took advantage of the distraction and hurried back onto the runway.

"Richard," I yelled as the music paused between songs. "Don't let her escape."

As the first few chords of "Rock You Like A Hurricane" blasted from the speakers, I pushed a redheaded model to the side and ran onto the runway with clipboard lady screaming at me to stop. The dark-haired model glanced behind her, and her eyes filled with panic as she spotted me giving chase. She hiked her skirt and hopped off the end of the runway. I followed. For a girl who seemed like she could blow away in a stiff breeze, she could run fast. She'd almost reached the back ballroom door when Richard dashed from the other side of the room and knocked her over. She tried to scramble up, but Richard sat on her back.

"Get off me," she shrieked, struggling underneath his weight.

I reached the pair and stopped to catch my breath. "Nice tackle."

Richard arched a brow. "I've watched football."

"Cut the music," clipboard lady said from the runway, where she leveled a finger at Richard and me. "You ruined my dress rehearsal."

The music stopped, and the models came out onto the runway, staring at the scene of Richard in his perfectly pressed lavender button-down shirt and black pants sitting on top of a model half his size. Christopher and Fern both ran over.

Christopher's face flushed red. "What are you doing? Get off her at once."

Richard held up a finger and ticked it back and forth like a metronome. "Not until we retrieve the diamonds."

"What are you talking about?" Christopher asked.

Richard leaned over the flailing girl, put one hand on each side of her head, and shook her like a Magic Eight Ball.

Clipboard lady and several of the models screamed. Christopher's mouth dropped open, and Fern swooned against me. Before I could tell Richard to stop, the first ring dropped from the model's hair. Then another and another and the room went silent.

Richard stopped shaking and picked up a diamond ring from the floor. "Does anyone have any questions now?"

The model raised her head from the floor. "I didn't know they were in there. Christopher said he added crystals to my hair. I had no idea they were actually diamond rings."

"That's not true," Christopher said, gaping at the girl on the ground. "I never said I added crystals to her hair."

"Who else could have done it?" Fern asked. "It certainly wasn't me. And the beehives were all your idea."

Christopher shook his head. "No, they were her idea."

Richard put his hands on his hips without getting off the model. "You expect us to believe that this model picked the hairstyles for the fashion show and managed to hide the diamond rings inside her own hair?"

"Stella," Christopher said, his voice now barely a whisper. "Tell them."

The girl didn't meet his gaze. "I had nothing to do with this."

The double doors opened, and Kate came inside followed by Detective Mike Reese and the scowling head of hotel security. All three paused when they saw Richard perched on top of the tiny model with several diamond rings scattered around her head.

Detective Reese stared at Richard, then at me, and shook his head slowly. "Why am I not surprised?"

CHAPTER 12

"**I** suppose that's that," Richard said as we made our way through the ballroom foyer on the basement level. He'd been peeved that Detective Reese had not wanted him to shake the remaining rings from the model's head. "I suppose Fern will do a fine job, but my way would have been faster."

The woman with the clipboard had declared the dress rehearsal to be over and had stalked back to the hair and makeup room with the rest of the models. I'd barely spoken to Detective Reese before he'd gone off to question Christopher in the hotel security office. I'd been proud of myself for acting normal around him. Well, as normal as could be expected after he walked in on my best friend pinning down a model and shaking diamonds out of her beehive. I felt a little disappointed that he hadn't said more when he saw me, but at least I hadn't embarrassed myself.

"Your face is still flushed," Kate said.

I put my fingers to my cheeks. "Flushed?"

"You turned red the second Reese walked in the door," Richard said. "Even I noticed from the floor."

I groaned. Great. So much for playing it cool.

"Don't worry." Kate patted my arm. "I doubt the detective noticed. He was too busy dragging Richard off that poor model."

"He did not drag me off. He merely assisted me in standing up. But he should have thanked me for trying to be thorough."

"You promise me you had nothing to do with him being here?" I asked Kate again as I dodged the one remaining ladder in the foyer.

She drew an X over her heart with one finger. "You know I didn't. Only a few minutes passed from when I left the room to when I ran into Reese and the security guard coming up in the elevator. Hotel security had already called the police."

I studied her with suspicion. "And the detective just happened to be the one assigned to the case?"

Kate shrugged. "The hotel may have mentioned that it was a bridal show and there were nosy wedding planners."

I closed my eyes. "Perfect."

"At least the show can go on." Kate glanced at her phone. "And we still have thirty minutes before the brides arrive."

"Thirty minutes?" I said. "We've barely done any setup."

We passed through the open double doors of the basement ballroom and I stopped. I shouldn't have been surprised by how dramatically the room had transformed during the half hour we'd been upstairs because it happened with every event setup, but the change still startled me.

Like all major events, this one had come together quickly at the end. The lighting stands had been tucked out of the way and now illuminated the ceiling with swirling patterns of pale pink and lavender light. The carpet had been cleared of all boxes and crates so we could walk freely down the middle of the room. The vendor displays on either side were finished and a string quartet sat tuning their instruments on the stage at the far end.

"Am I seeing things or is that wedding planner offering Botox?" Richard said to me as we passed Brides by Brianna.

"Interested?" Kate asked.

Richard gave her a venomous look. "I would as soon get Botox at a wedding show as I'd get a massage at the airport."

"Well, I'll bet you she has a line out the door for the entire day," Kate said.

Richard sniffed. "There are some things one does not do in public."

I was with Richard on this one. If I ever got to the point where I felt the need to shoot toxins into my face, I certainly wouldn't pick the middle of the Hotel W ballroom as the place to do it. But, then again, I also knew about the powerful lure of freebies and that some of the brides at the show came to drink as much Champagne, eat as much free cake, and collect as many free gifts as possible.

"I wish we had something as tempting as Botox to give away," Kate said.

"We have the chocolates covered in gold dust," I reminded her.

She held up her two hands like scales. "Botox. Chocolates. Which would you stand in line for?"

"You forgot the gold dust," I said.

Kate eyed me. "Unless we're offering to spray the brides in gold dust from head to toe, I don't think there's much competition."

I waved to Tammy from Tamara's Flowers, who still wore her apron and stood misting her flower garland from a green spray bottle. She waved back.

"Since when are there blue carnations?" Richard asked once we'd passed the florist's booth.

"Since she painted them," Kate said in a lowered voice.

Richard wrinkled his nose. "Well, I hope all that misting doesn't make her spray-painted flowers run."

"Be nice you two," I said. "It's her first show."

"At least she's set up," Kate said as we reached the Wedding Belles display. Although the gold branches were no longer piled on the floor and now created a lush, leafy canopy over the entire ten-foot square space, our gold bar stood bare save the orchid arrangement on the far right side. A light sprinkling of gold paint from the branches dusted the floor. "Our space is a ghost town."

"It won't be once we set out the chocolates." I hurried behind the bar to where my bags had been hidden. I pulled out a pair of gold and white cake stands and placed them on the bar. "See? Better already."

Richard stood back and tapped a finger to his chin. "How many more cake stands do you have under there? A hundred?"

"I have these." I produced a pair of three-tiered dessert displays ornamented with gilded birds and set them next to the cake stands.

"And?" Richard said.

I stood up and put my hands on my hips. "And the chocolates to go on them."

"This can't compete with Botox Barbie down there," Kate said, flailing an arm in the direction of our competition.

"She's right," Richard said. "As ridiculous as I find jabbing needles in people's foreheads in public, you can't deny that the idea is good for buzz."

I reached under the bar for one of the boxes of gold-dusted chocolates in the shape of jewels and resisted the urge to slam it on top. "Buzz? Since when did being a good wedding planner become about creating buzz?"

"Since forever." Richard came up to the bar and sat on one of the stools. "But now the buzz isn't about the actual weddings you plan, it's about the hype. The fake wedding you design for a styled shoot, the absurdly elaborate tablescape at a wedding show that no bride could afford, the birthday dinner you throw for yourself so you can post perfect Instagram pics. Buzz, buzz, buzz."

I made a face. "Fake, fake, fake." Richard knew how much I detested the idea of designing fake events for photos, even though it seemed to be the fashionable thing to do. I maintained that I didn't have time to make up a fake wedding and book a photographer to shoot it. Not when I was busy planning actual weddings.

"Smoke and mirrors, darling. Smoke and mirrors." He twisted around on his stool and gestured to the woman in the lab coat across the room. "Sadly, now the smoke and mirrors have needles and liability waivers."

"We can't compete with that. No bride will bother coming over here now." I felt tears pricking the back of my eyes. What was wrong with me today?

Richard slipped off his stool and walked around to me, draping an arm around my shoulder. "Of course they will. Not everyone getting married has the skin of a fifty-year-old."

"I have an idea." Kate tapped away at her phone.

Richard and I exchanged glances. Kate's ideas usually involved hot guys, skimpy clothes, and cocktails. I didn't see how any of those could help us now.

Kate tore her eyes from her phone long enough to meet mine. "Trust me."

Before I could protest, Lorinda rushed up to me with Fern only a few steps behind her. "You did it. You got my diamonds back!"

Her excitement snapped me out of my funk. "That was fast. I thought it would take a lot longer to pick them out of that girl's hair."

"I might have used Richard's technique to speed things along," Fern said.

"You mean you shook them out?" I asked.

Fern shrugged. "Maybe once or twice. But I got them all out."

Lorinda held up a black velvet roll of fabric. "And just in time, too."

Over her head, I could see that brides were already gathering in the lobby. Where had the time gone? I felt like I'd arrived a few minutes ago, and already it was showtime.

"You need to change." Richard eyed my jeans and T-shirt.

I glanced down at myself. I'd forgotten that I still had on my set-up clothes.

"Good thing. You've got gold all over the bottom of your jeans." Kate pointed to the layer of gold dust on my calves. Then she pointed to Richard's pants legs. "You, too."

"Perfect." Richard wiped at his pants and came away with gold on his palms.

I pointed to the gilded canopy of greenery above our heads. "It's from the branches that Buster and Mack spray-painted gold. I must have brushed up against them. And it got all over the carpet."

Fern kicked a leg up behind him. "The bottoms of my shoes are gold. How fun!"

"Don't worry. Brides won't notice your legs," Kate said to Richard.

"I don't care about that," Richard said. "These are Prada pants, and they aren't supposed to be gold. My days of wearing gold pants are long over."

"Richard in gold pants." Kate smiled. "Now that's something I'd like to see."

"Not on your life." Richard made a face at her, then walked off.

"Come on." Fern scooped my garment bag from where I'd hung it off the edge of the bar. "You can change and I'll fix your hair."

I put a hand to my ponytail as Fern pushed me out from behind the bar.

"Yes, for heaven's sake do something with her hair," Kate said.

I glanced back as Fern pulled me away from the Wedding Belles space.

"Don't worry," Kate said. "By the time you come back, this booth will be a bride magnet. Trust me."

Knowing Kate the way I did, I wasn't so sure if her idea of attracting brides would fit our brand. Or be legal.

CHAPTER 13

Once I'd changed into my sleeveless turquoise sheath dress and black peep-toe heels, Fern draped a black smock around my shoulders and steered me onto a stool. The "Hair by Fernando" space consisted of a square silver mirror suspended below his sign, a stool for brides to sit on, and a table that held his brushes, sprays, clips, and bobby pins. A pair of magazine covers of models he'd styled had been blown up and placed on metal easels to flank the space. It was simple and clean, which seemed like the complete opposite of Fern's dramatic personal style. But, then again, Fern didn't need a lot to draw in brides since his personality and wardrobe already filled the room.

Fern's space stood on the left side of the room near the entrance doors, almost as far away from Christopher's space as possible. I wondered what the show organizers would do with the disgraced hairstylist's booth now. Fern couldn't work fast enough to do hair for the several hundred brides who'd be streaming through the doors in a matter of minutes. I could only imagine the stampede once brides realized there was only one hairdresser doing free updos.

Fern pulled the black elastic from my hair so that it spilled over my shoulders and down my back. "Let's do something with this perpetual ponytail look you have going on."

"I don't always wear it in a ponytail," I said. "I put it in a bun on wedding days."

He patted my shoulder. "Way to shake things up, girl."

"Were you surprised about Christopher?" I asked.

Fern tugged a round brush through my hair. "Well, you might have noticed that he wasn't my favorite colleague."

Talk about an understatement. "Yep. I noticed."

"But between you and me." Fern leaned close to my ear. "I'm surprised he had the brains to pull it off. He might have been somewhat attractive." Another understatement. "But I never pegged him for being clever."

In the reflection of Fern's mirror, I spotted Detective Reese as he walked into the ballroom. He wore jeans topped with a sky-blue button-down shirt and a brown blazer that was just rumpled enough to look cool. He was one of those infuriating men who looked good in just about anything he put on without even trying. He stopped and surveyed the room until he saw me, then he crossed over to us in a few strides. "Just the woman I hoped to find."

"Well, that sounds promising," Fern muttered so only I could hear him.

"How can I help you, Detective?" I asked, trying to keep my voice steady. *Act nonchalant*, I told myself. *Pretend like he doesn't faze you at all. Did he grow his hair out a bit?*

Reese took a small notebook out of his blazer pocket and tapped his pen on it. "How long has it been?"

"Since?" I said, even though I knew perfectly well what he meant. *That's right. Play it cool.*

"Since you've shown up at one of my investigations?" he said. "A month?"

"More like two," I said a bit too quickly. Fern yanked at my hair as he pulled a strand from one side to the top. I recognized the signal.

Reese grinned. "Two, huh? Well, it's been a pretty dull two months then."

"We've all been staying out of trouble," Fern said.

Reese studied him. "Somehow I doubt that."

"You're so bad." Fern swatted at him with his hairbrush. "Tell him he's bad, Annabelle."

I glared at Fern in the mirror, but he didn't see me. Now who was making a fool of themselves? I tried to crane my neck around, but Fern yanked me back by my hair.

"How did you get assigned to this case? Don't you do homicides?" I asked Reese. I caught his eyes in the mirror and tried hard not to notice how they deepened from hazel to a moss green.

"We had a terror threat across town this morning so they called me in on my day off."

"Sorry about that," I said.

He shrugged and grinned. "I've had worse assignments." He cleared his throat. "You're one of the witnesses to the crime, correct?"

"Kate and I were a few feet away when it happened."

Reese scribbled in his notebook. "Did you see anything?"

"Well, the lights were out so no," I said. "But we heard fumbling with the jewelry cabinet and then Lorinda yelled. Or it may have been the other way around."

"Did you hear the burglar when they ran off?"

I started to shake my head, but Fern held it straight as he fastened my hair at the top of my head. "I didn't but Botox Barbie heard someone run by her."

"Botox Barbie?" Reese asked, grinning.

"Sorry," I said. "I mean Brianna. She's the wedding planner doing Botox injections in her booth."

"You can't miss her." Fern fluffed my half-up half-down hair around my shoulders. "She's extremely blond."

Reese met my eyes in the mirror again and held them. "Is there anything else you'd like to tell me?"

Like that I think your longer hair is sexy and I'd love to run my hands through it? I rubbed my palms on the front of my legs as I forced myself not to stare at him. "Not that I can think of. It happened pretty fast."

Fern unfurled the smock from my shoulders. "You're all done. I've saved you from Ponytail Purgatory."

I mentally added Fern to my list of people to kill if Washington ever opted for a purge.

"Okay. I guess I'll talk to the Botox girl then." Reese leaned in and tapped his notebook on my knee. "I like your hair down. You should wear it like this more often."

"Don't think I don't tell her that all the time," Fern called after him.

I stood up, then pivoted and smacked Fern on the arm. "Ponytail purgatory?"

He rubbed the spot where I'd hit him. "What? He said he liked your hair, didn't he? He came over to talk to you, am I right?"

"About the case," I said.

"Frankly, I don't know why everyone's making such a big deal about these diamonds." Fern folded the black smock over his stool. "I know they're part of Lorinda's display, but it isn't like they're real."

"I'm sorry, what?"

"The diamonds I fished out of that model's hair were not real," Fern said. "If there are two things I know it's hair and gemstones. Well, I know more than two things, but I definitely know jewelry. And those were not genuine diamonds."

I stared at Fern. If he was right, none of this made any sense.

CHAPTER 14

"Where are we going?" Fern asked as he hurried behind me, weaving through booths and around people. I passed the Brides by Brianna booth and saw her being questioned by Detective Reese. I ignored the fact that she had her hand on his arm and his back pressed up against the table of Botox needles. A part of me hoped he'd get a needle in the backside for smiling back at her.

"To see those diamonds," I said. As I approached the Goodman & Sons display, I slowed to a stop.

"Well, that's a new approach for you," Fern said.

The Wedding Belles area had transformed from simple and elegant to gawk-worthy. Club music emanated from somewhere behind the bar and provided the beat for a pair of hunky guys in skin-tight black T-shirts who were tossing bottles of booze in the air. Kate stood in front of the bar arranging gold-flecked martini glasses into an impressive tower.

"What's all this?" I asked.

Kate swept her arms open. "This is our bride catnip."

I had to admit that I had a hard time taking my eyes off the men behind the bar with their very large and very tanned biceps.

"We may not be able to deaden their foreheads," Kate said. "But we can give them some eye candy and cocktails."

"Boys and booze." Fern nodded his appreciation. "Two great things that go great together."

"Do I want to ask how you found these guys so quickly?" I said.

"Kurt and Alex are craft bartenders downtown," Kate said. "I've known them for years. You know how you go home after weddings and crawl into bed? Well, I go have a cocktail or two."

"She's one of our best customers." The brawny blond from behind the bar said and winked at me.

I did not find this surprising in the least. "So what are we serving?"

Kate clapped her hands. "They're creating a custom cocktail for us called the Wedding Belle. Don't you love it?"

I tried not to cringe. It was one thing for our brides to have custom cocktails with cutesy names but I could have gone years without having a drink named after my company. The dark-haired bartender passed me a martini glass across the bar with a light blue concoction inside and a curl of lemon peel dangling from the lip of the glass. "Try it. It's something new and something blue."

"Look at you with the wedding lingo." Fern batted his eyes at the bartender.

I took a sip. The drink was good. I took another sip. Very good.

"Kate asked us to make it a little sweet and a little tart," the blond bartender said.

"Like us," Kate said. "Get it?"

"Subtle." I passed the drink to Fern.

"Don't mind if I do," he said, then downed the drink in one gulp.

"Another?" the blond beefcake asked.

"That's a hard no." It would not pay for me to be tipsy when brides started streaming through the doors. Plus, I needed to keep my wits about me if Lorinda's diamonds really were fakes.

"I'll have another," Fern said. "And don't go light on the liquor."

I tugged on his jacket. "You can't get drunk. I need you to inspect those diamond rings again on the down low."

Fern giggled. "The down low?"

"You know what I mean." I jerked my head in the direction of the Goodman & Sons booth where Lorinda stood wiping off the top of her glass jewelry case. "Casually admire the rings and see if they're real."

Fern sighed. "Then can I have another cocktail?"

I gave him a push. "Yes, but one more and I'm cutting you off. If you drink too much, you start calling all the brides tramps."

"He does that anyway," Kate said.

"Au contraire." Fern shook a finger at her. "I call them all hussies. I only call them tramps when I drink."

I watched as Fern sidled up to Lorinda's jewelry case and began gushing over the rings. His act looked extremely convincing, probably because it wasn't much of an act. Fern was like a bird when it came to shiny objects.

"What's this?" Brianna's voice pulled my attention away from Fern. Her hands were on her hips, but her eyes were on our bartenders. "I thought you were giving out chocolates."

"Change of plans." Kate leaned her elbows back against the bar and stared at Brianna. "How did you know what we were doing anyway?"

Brianna arched a brow. "I do my homework, and I always know my competition."

I exchanged a glance with Kate. "I thought you'd never heard of us."

Brianna opened her mouth, then shut it again. She turned to leave and walked into Detective Reese. She spluttered and giggled and clutched his arms a little too hard before walking back to her booth.

Kate smiled when she recognized Reese. "Fancy a drink, Detective?"

Reese took in our booth with an amused expression.

I felt my face flush. "Don't look at me. This is all Kate."

"Guilty." Kate curtsied.

"It makes a statement. I'll give that to you," he said.

"So how's the questioning going?" I asked, flicking my eyes over to Fern trying on a ring and holding his fingers up in the air. No one could say he wasn't playing his part to the hilt. I didn't want to tell Reese what Fern had told me until I was absolutely certain.

Detective Reese stepped closer to me. "Not bad. It's mostly a formality for the report."

I tried to think of something clever to say to prolong the conversation, but my mind went blank. All I could think of was how close we were standing to each other, and my pulse quickened. Kate backed away, leaving me standing alone with the detective.

"I wanted to ask you something." He lowered his voice and leaned into me, resting a hand on the small of my back. "Do you remember the last time we saw each other at your apartment? I wanted to ask if—"

"Mission accomplished," Fern said as he walked back over to me.

The detective dropped his hand from my back.

"Wait," I said, not sure if I was talking more to Fern or Reese.

"Yes, don't go." Fern grabbed Reese's elbow. "You're going to want to hear this, too."

I tried to meet the detective's eyes to mouth an apology or an explanation, but he focused on Fern.

"What do I need to hear?" he asked.

"That I was right." Fern said. "Those diamond rings we found in the model's hair are as fake as Kate's winter tan."

CHAPTER 15

D etective Reese tilted his head as he stared at Fern. "So you think that the diamond rings that were stolen were fake?"

Fern shook his head. "I think the diamond rings we found were fake."

"Meaning?" I said.

Fern glanced behind him at Lorinda. He had nothing to worry about. There was no chance she could hear us over the music coming from behind the bar. "I tried on the same ring two times today. The first time, before the blackout, the diamond was genuine. The second time, right now, it was fake."

"You're positive?" Reese asked.

Fern leveled a withering stare at him. "I know my jewelry, sweetie. Those were different stones. I'm not saying there aren't some very convincing synthetic stones on the market but these are more along the lines of cubic zirconia, so it's not hard to tell if you know what you're looking for."

"I don't understand," I said. "Why would there be two sets of diamonds?"

"And bad luck for the thief who snatched the wrong ones,"

Fern said. "Is it still a crime if what you steal isn't worth anything?"

"I'm thinking yes," I said to Fern under my breath.

Detective Reese pulled out his notebook and began scanning his notes. "The real question is where are the real diamonds if the ones we recovered aren't real?"

"Richard," Kate called. "Come have a cocktail!"

I turned around to see Richard walk up holding a floor sweeper. He glanced at his Gucci watch. "Brides will be coming through those doors in five minutes. I don't think now is the time for drinking."

Kate held out a frothy blue drink in a martini glass. "It's the perfect time. I promise you it will take the edge right off."

"Off him or the brides?" Fern asked, and I hushed him.

Richard waved off the drink. "I popped over to bring you this." He propelled the floor sweeper forward. "Unless you want every bride who walks by your space to leave dragging gold dust with her."

I took the sweeper and ran it over the section of carpet with the most gold covering it. Some of the dust vanished but a good deal remained. "This may take more than a sweeper."

Richard frowned. "Well, I didn't bring my carpet shampooer."

I pointed to the sweeper. "Wait. Did you bring this with you?"

"Of course," Richard said. "Hotels never have enough brooms, and finding someone to run a vacuum at the last minute is next to impossible, so I brought my own cleaning supplies."

I reminded myself to have Richard over to my apartment more often. With his supplies.

"How did you get gold all over the floor?" Reese asked, stepping closer to the gold patch that covered most of our space.

I pointed above our heads. "See all those leaves? Buster and Mack spray painted them and some of the paint got onto the floor."

"Leaves don't grow gold," Mack called over from his booth,

where he stood placing the final few palm fronds into a large arrangement. "Not that I'm complaining about the metallic craze. It could be worse."

"We all got it on our pants and shoes earlier," Richard said. "Luckily, I also brought stain-remover wipes so my Prada pants were saved."

"And I wasn't wearing pants." Kate gestured to her short shirt and exposed bare legs.

"I wonder." I pulled Reese to the side. "Can you find out if Christopher and the model have gold dust on their shoes?"

His expression seemed confused, then he nodded. "I can do that. Let me call my guys."

While the detective walked away from the Wedding Belles booth and pulled out his phone, Buster and Mack joined us.

Kate swept her arms wide. "Care for a drink?"

Both men, confirmed teetotalers, declined her offer but gazed appreciatively at the bartenders flipping bottles and pouring their blue concoction into gold-flecked glasses.

"This is a departure from the original design, no?" Buster asked me.

"You could say that," I said. "Kate amped it up a bit."

"We have to compete with the likes of Botox Barbie over there." Kate gestured to Brianna's booth with her drink, and a bit of blue liquid sloshed over the side of the glass.

"That girl?" Mack said. "You don't need to worry about her. She doesn't have a clue what she's doing."

"You know her?" I asked.

"She came into the studio for a 'meet and greet.'" Buster made air quotes with his fingers. "Claimed she wanted to get to know us but then spent the entire time asking questions about other planners, mostly you two."

"Really?" Kate glared in Brianna's direction.

"You two have come up so fast that now you're the ones to beat," Buster said.

It felt nice to think of all our hard work paying off but not so nice to think that we were now the planners that other people wanted to knock off. So much for our moment in the sun.

"She asked us to design her booth for the show," Mack said. "Can you imagine? And she's never even sent us a scrap of business."

"I doubt she has a scrap of business," Richard said. "Smoke and mirrors, I tell you."

"Smoke and mirrors and Botox," I reminded him. "But why would she make a point of saying she'd never heard of us earlier?"

"Maybe she has memory issues. Have you seen how blond she is?" Fern asked. "And that's a bottle job, too."

"Hey." Kate tapped her foot on the floor. "Don't knock all blondes."

"Not you, darling." Fern walked over and fluffed her hair. "You never let your roots go."

I wasn't sure if that was the compliment Fern meant it to be and could tell by Kate's face that she wasn't sure, either.

"Annabelle?" Detective Reese tugged on my elbow.

I followed him out of earshot of the others. "So, was my hunch right?"

"You were right. Neither Christopher nor the model had gold paint on them. Not the bottom of their shoes, not their pants, not her dress."

"So neither of them could have been near the jewelry case to steal the diamonds."

He shook his head and gave me a half grin. "Would it do any good to tell you to leave the crime-solving to the police?"

I returned his smile. "What do you think?"

CHAPTER 16

"**N**ot only is there no direct evidence that the hairdresser stole the rings, he swears up and down that he had nothing to do with it," Detective Reese told me.

"Since my theory that he snuck through the back of his booth to the Goodman & Sons booth is shot, maybe he didn't take the rings," I said.

"The fake rings," Reese corrected me.

I held up a finger. "But Fern swears that the rings he looked at before the blackout weren't fake. He's sure there are two sets of rings."

The detective cast his eyes around the room. "Okay. Then where are they?"

I glanced around me. The first few brides were being let in through the tall double doors at the front of the room. They carried canvas tote bags with the show's blue logo splashed across the side, and I knew they would soon be filling the bags with everything from pamphlets to business cards to favors. I hoped they wouldn't try to make off with our martini glasses. Or our bartenders.

"Well, if the diamonds in the model's beehive were fake and the guards have searched every person leaving the ballroom, then the rings must still be here."

Reese watched the brides entering with their new totes and groaned. "Don't tell me we're going to have to search every bride when she leaves."

I agreed that this was not an appealing prospect. Not only would it take forever but the brides were sure to raise a fuss.

"You planning to join me?" Kate asked as she came up to me. "I don't know if I can sell all these brides by myself."

Richard and Fern had disappeared, no doubt off to their own booths. Buster and Mack stood in front of their elaborate tablescape ready to talk to potential clients. Our hunky bartenders were flashing gold cocktail shakers and preening for the small group of brides who'd already gathered. I didn't have much time before I needed to begin passing out our cards and giving our spiel.

"Two seconds," I said to Kate.

Reese shook his head. "I should let you go. And I should remind you which one of us is the detective."

"Well then, Detective, I suggest you talk to Brianna again. She's the only person we found who heard someone hurrying past her in the dark." I leaned back to check out the Brides by Brianna booth. "And it doesn't appear that any brides have accepted her needle-in-the-forehead offer yet so she's free to talk."

"Thanks." Reese did not seem pleased by this information, and I felt pleased that he hadn't fallen under the blond bridal consultant's spell.

I joined Kate and pulled a small stack of my cards out of my dress pocket. "It seems like our boys and booze are more of a draw then Brianna's dead foreheads."

Kate gave our bartenders a thumbs-up as they tossed two cocktail shakers in the air to each other, then poured the contents out into a row of martini glasses. The cluster of brides around the bar clapped. "What did you expect? These girls may be engaged, but they're not dead. A cocktail from a hot boy will win out every time versus a needle in the face."

"It serves her right for lying about knowing us."

"Maybe she's too ditzy to remember that she'd heard of us. Fern did say all that hair bleaching could fry her brain."

I rolled my eyes. "I'd take anything Fern tells you with a grain of salt. Or a sack of it. I think she's an opportunist. She says what she needs to say at any given moment."

A bride approached us holding a blue drink. "I'll take her," Kate said to me, then turned on her brightest smile for the potential client. "I see you have your something blue already."

The girl giggled. "These are so yummy. This is my second."

Already? I hoped this girl signed contracts as fast as she downed cocktails.

"Developing signature drink concepts is one of the services we offer in our full planning package," Kate said. "Can I tell you more about full planning?"

"Well, I'm actually getting married in Ohio, but I wondered if I could have the recipe for this drink."

Kate's face froze, and I stifled a laugh. Strike one for brides. I hoped this wasn't another bad omen for the day. I glanced over at Brianna, who stood talking to Reese. I averted my gaze so I wouldn't feel irritated watching her flirt with him. Then something occurred to me. "She made it all up."

"What?" Kate asked.

"Who made up the drink?" the Ohio bride asked.

"Not the drink." I patted the bride's arm. "Brianna. Brianna lied."

"Who's Brianna?" The bride sounded slightly buzzed and very confused.

"We already went over this, Annabelle," Kate said in a low voice.

"Not about that." I clapped to focus her attention. "About the blackout. She didn't hear anyone running past her. I'll bet she made that up for the attention or to feel important or to sound more interesting."

"I'm sorry." The bride eyes moved from me to Kate. "What blackout? Is that the name of the drink? I thought it was called the Wedding Belle."

Kate peered down the row at Brianna who chose that moment to toss her head back in a fake laugh. "You might be right."

"I'm sure I'm right." The bride took another sip and glanced back over her shoulder at the gold bar. "The bartender said 'the Wedding Belle.' Oh, is that your company name, too? How fun!"

I ignored the bride. "It makes sense. Especially since she was the only person who was adamant about hearing a person rushing past."

"Whipped cream vodka, blue curacao, drop of lemon juice, lemon twist," Kate said to the bride while steering her out of our area with one hand and taking the empty martini glass with the other. "So if that's true, the only person who had any contact with the thief was Lorinda."

I focused on the jeweler, who stood a few feet away from us showing off her rings to a pair of women. "If the rings were fake, at least one set of them, what's to say the thief wasn't fake either?"

CHAPTER 17

"What do you mean the thief was fake?" Kate pulled me a few feet farther away from Goodman & Sons Jewelers. "You think Lorinda made it up?"

"It's clear that Lorinda was in on it because otherwise why wouldn't a second-generation diamond expert notice the rings are fakes? Originally I thought she'd arranged for the burglary but it actually makes sense that there never was a burglary. Think about it. No one else had any encounter with a thief who supposedly ran up in the dark, snatched a tray full of rings, and left. Doesn't that strike you as odd?"

Kate set the empty martini glass on a nearby cocktail table. "So you think she made up the thief and took her own jewelry? But where did she put it, and how did a complete set of replica diamonds end up in the beehive of a model?"

"I haven't worked all of that out yet. And I hope I'm wrong." I chanced a glance at Lorinda as she laughed with a bride and her mother. She didn't seem like the criminal type and, as far as I could tell, she had no motive to fake a robbery. To tell the truth, I wasn't fully comfortable with the idea of Lorinda setting up the crime. For one, she'd been the person to ask me to find the rings.

Would she do that if she'd planned the heist herself? And for another, I liked her. She was a fellow female businesswoman, and she seemed sensible. That wasn't always easy to come by in the wedding world.

"Where did Detective Reese go?" I asked.

I scanned the room, now filled with brides. Some had come in pairs, some had mothers with them, and some had brought reluctant grooms. I could barely see the heads of our bartenders over the crowd that had accumulated around our bar.

"I'm going to go find the detective," I told Kate. "I need to tell him my theory and see if he can poke some holes in it."

Kate clutched my arm. "You're leaving me alone?"

"Why are you complaining? The brides are busy with the show." I gestured at the girls cheering the bartenders as the two men shook their cocktail shakers in unison.

"What happens if they get rowdy?"

"Well, what happens when you get rowdy at a bar?" I asked, knowing that this probably happened more often than I wanted to know.

"I go home with one of the bartenders," she said. "I don't think that's such a good idea here."

"Let's hope it doesn't come to that." I pointed to a girl dropping an empty martini glass in her tote bag. "Those glasses are rentals, right?"

"Why do people think that everything at a bridal show is up for grabs?" Kate headed off to fish the martini glass out of the bride's bag while I snaked my way through the ever-growing crowd.

I waved at the makeup artist who was misting a setting spray over a bride's face. Her line for complimentary "lashes and lips" held at least a dozen people. I cut through the line and passed by Tammy the florist whose voice had gone up several octaves as she pitched herself to brides. I understood her nerves. I'd felt faint and nauseated the first time we'd done a bridal show. I gave a cursory glance to Brianna as I walked by. She had what appeared to be a mother of the bride in the Botox chair and a handful of brides pausing to watch. Brianna's smile appeared unnaturally bright and forced, and she made a point not to notice me.

I rounded the corner of the drape wall and headed down the next row of displays. A videographer who looked too young to shave, a DJ behind a raised metal booth wearing oversized headphones, a wedding cake baker passing out samples of chocolate hazelnut cake and vanilla sponge with Grand Marnier. But no detective.

I passed the cosmetic dentist with his two pretty assistants in crisp lab coats who were distributing coupons for teeth whitening. Right next to them, Richard stood behind his towering display of confections with a handsome waiter in front holding a silver tray with cocktail napkins. A group of women loaded their napkins with sweets while Richard passed them his card. He motioned for me to join him behind his table.

"Of course you can do a brunch for your reception. We do a fabulous sweet and savory crepe station."

One of the women dabbed at her mouth with a lavender cocktail napkin. "I thought more along the lines of waffles with flavored syrups."

Richard's face froze and his gaze moved to the woman next to her. "And when is your wedding?"

"I'm a bridesmaid."

He pulled back his cards. "Enjoy the show, ladies. Don't miss the teeth whitening next door."

They wandered off, and Richard put the back of his hand to his forehead. "Waffles? Does it look like I'm running a Waffle House here? Do I seem like I've ever set foot inside a Waffle House?"

I shook my head. "I'm surprised you even knew they existed."

"I have to tell you, Annabelle, I'm not so sure this crowd is our clientele. I've had one bride asking about a cookout with hotdogs and hamburgers, one who asked if I could recreate Chick-fil-A nuggets as an hors d'oeuvre, and now Miss Waffle House."

"So far we've had an Ohio bride who wanted our drink recipe and another who tried to steal the glassware."

Richard slumped forward on his elbows. "I'm worn out, and it's only been thirty minutes."

"Has Detective Reese passed by here?"

"I think I saw him heading toward Christopher's empty booth. Why?"

I told Richard my theory regarding Lorinda and my misgivings about it. "I can't think of why she would do it. She doesn't have motive."

"Money," Richard said. "The oldest motive there is. She'd receive an insurance payout if the rings were stolen."

"But she has a successful business. Goodman & Sons is one of the biggest names in town."

"Maybe, but I know old Mr. Goodman is tough on her. He always wanted a boy and never got one, hence the company name. But it isn't only her he's awful to. He's never satisfied with anything anyone does. I'm sure she's under a lot of pressure to increase profits."

"How do you know all this?" I asked.

"I catered that party for them, remember?" Richard said, pulling out his cell phone. "I'm sure I have pictures in my phone. We did all the stations themed after a gemstone. My idea, of course. The entire extended family showed up and the old man didn't appear to like any of them very much. The feeling seemed mutual from the whispering I heard. Not that I blame them."

Knowing this made me even more sympathetic toward Lorinda. I couldn't imagine trying to live up to a father who always wanted you to be a boy.

"So receiving a big insurance payout but still having the diamonds to sell would mean more profits?"

"I'm sure." Richard scrolled through the photos on his phone.

"All she'd have to do is report that the recovered diamonds were fake after the show. Maybe claim she didn't have time to inspect them in all the hustle and bustle. She'd be able to move the real rings off the property without the tight security since the rings had been found. It would be pretty believable."

I eyed Richard. "Have you ever thought about becoming a master thief?"

"All the time, Annabelle. All the time." He held up his phone screen. "Here's a photo from the party. We did one station all in green to represent emeralds. All the food was green, the linen was green, and the flowers were green."

I inspected the photo and tried not to make a face at the sight of all the green food. "That's green all right."

He took back his phone and flipped to another image. "And the diamond station. All white, naturally."

He passed me the photo of a buffet table covered in a shimmery white cloth with a massive white floral arrangement in the center dripping with crystals.

"Who's that behind the table?" I asked, pointing to a dark-haired girl in the background.

Richard glanced at the photo. "Some niece, I think. The entire family shares the same features—dark hair, pale. Very Morticia Addams."

"Well, either we have a serious doppelganger situation going on here or that girl in the picture is the model who had all the diamonds in her hair."

CHAPTER 18

"**I** knew I recognized her from somewhere." Richard snapped his fingers.

"So Lorinda and the model were in cahoots. Now it's all coming together."

"That pretty-boy hairdresser may not have known anything after all," Richard said over the buzzing of conversation and strains of string music from across the room. "He never seemed bright enough to hatch a jewelry heist to me, anyway."

I searched the sea of women and the occasional bewildered groom. "I need to find Reese and tell him. Do you mind if I steal your phone?"

"As long as you bring it back. I may need it to send out SOS messages if these Waffle House brides continue."

"Sorry," I mouthed as I left him with a stunned expression on his face at an approaching couple wearing matching burgundy and yellow Redskins jerseys. I wound my way through the crowd, jumping up every so often to peer over the heads. No Reese. Where had he gone?

I followed the thumping music and cheers back to the Wedding Belles display, which was now body-to-body with brides. I couldn't even find Kate until I stood on my tiptoes and spotted her blond hair behind the bar. I pushed my way through the crowd until I reached her.

I held up Richard's phone. "I found a new clue."

Kate pointed to her ear and shrugged. I realized she couldn't hear me over the music and the chanting brides. "The drinks are a hit," she yelled. "The guys can't pour them fast enough so I'm helping." She had a row of cocktail shakers lined up in front of her and a bottle of vodka in one hand and blue curacao in the other. She poured in the liquors. "Can you add the ice?"

I slipped Richard's phone in my pocket and wiggled behind the bar. My revelation could wait a few minutes. After all, I was here to promote the company, not solve crimes. I grabbed the metal scoop in the ice bucket and added ice to the cocktail shakers, causing some of the liquid to splash out the top. "Oops."

"Don't worry." Kate clamped the tops on the cocktail shakers and slid them down the bar to our shirtless bartenders. "It takes practice to add the perfect amount."

My eyes searched for a cloth to wipe up the spill, and I felt the gears in my brain clicking into place. Where had I seen someone else wiping up a spill? Lorinda. She'd been cleaning up water from the vase of flowers on her display. And if I remembered correctly, the spill had happened after the robbery. What if the spill wasn't a spill from the vase being jostled but water that overflowed the vase once something was added to it?

I peered over the sea of heads to Lorinda's display and spotted the vase, a white bubble bowl. Opaque enough so you couldn't see inside and large enough to hold plenty of diamonds along with the flower stems.

"I think I know where the diamonds are," I said to Kate and motioned to the jewelry case.

Kate tilted her head to one side. "I thought those were the fake ones."

"Not inside the case. On top."

Both of Kate's eyebrows went up, then her eyes caught something behind me. "Weren't you looking for Detective Reese?"

I turned around and saw the detective standing at the back of our crowd, his arms crossed and a crooked grin on his face. I waved both arms at him so he'd see me. He waved a single finger in response.

"I've got to go tell him what I found out about the model and the vase."

"I have no idea what you're talking about, but I'm right behind you," Kate said.

We pushed our way through the throng of thirsty and boisterous brides until we reached Reese.

He grinned. "That's quite a crowd you've got. I'm surprised no one's dancing on top of the bar yet."

"It's a bit more interactive than we expected," I said. "I've been searching all over for you."

"I've been avoiding your colleague." He glanced over his shoulder in the direction of Brianna's Botox booth. "She's . . . a lot."

"Not in the mood for a forehead full of toxins?" Kate asked.

"Among other things," Reese said.

I couldn't help feeling a wave of pleasure that the ditzy blonde hadn't charmed him. "Well, I'm pretty sure she lied about hearing the thief running past her."

"I agree," Reese said.

"You do?" I thought I'd have to lay out my reasoning to convince him.

He nodded. "She displayed obvious signs of deception when she told me her story and it changed from one telling to the next."

"Well, good," I said. "That means you might believe my theory that there was no burglar at all."

Reese took a step closer to me. "I'm listening."

I laid out my theory, showing him the iPhone photo and explaining about the connection between the model and Lorinda.

He cocked his head to one side and studied me for a moment. "Not bad, Annabelle. It seems like I need to bring a couple of ladies in for questioning."

Kate paled. "Not us, right? Because I don't think it's safe for us to leave the bartenders alone with this crowd."

"Not you," Reese reassured her.

"But you haven't heard the best part yet," I said. "I know where the diamonds are hidden. At least I think I know where the diamonds are hidden."

I pulled the detective behind me through the crowd with Kate following. I tried not to notice how nice his hand felt, warm and solid. Before we reached Lorinda's display, he maneuvered his fingers so that his enveloped mine. I felt my pulse quicken and hoped he wouldn't notice.

"Annabelle, Kate." Lorinda smiled when she saw us approach and faltered only slightly when she noticed me hand-in-hand with Detective Reese.

I dropped Reese's hand. "I'm so sorry, Lorinda." I took the pink roses out of her vase and laid them, dripping, on the glass of her display case.

She stepped back as water dripped onto her shoes. "What are you doing?"

I flipped the vase upside down and water gushed down over the case and the carpet below. Kate jumped back as water splattered all of us. I shook the vase harder, and a torrent of diamond rings fell out, clattering onto the jewelry case.

"Oh, now I understand what you were talking about." Kate thumped me on the back. "Nicely done, boss."

Lorinda's face darkened, and she set her mouth in a hard line.

Reese pulled out his phone and called for backup, then took Lorinda by the arm. "You need to come with me."

"Should we stay here?" I asked as a uniformed officer walked up and began gathering the diamonds in an evidence bag.

"Definitely." Reese paused in front of me. "I'm going to take her to the squad car, then come back in and take statements." He leaned close. "Don't even think of running out on me."

"I'll be right here." My voice came out much breathier than I'd intended.

After Reese and Lorinda left, Kate turned to me. "And you said bridal shows were all the same."

CHAPTER 19

"That was, without a doubt, the most memorable bridal show in history," Richard said as he leaned against the sleek black bar in the hotel's lobby, club music pulsing in the background. Oversized geometric crystals studded the sides of the bar and created a stark contrast with the intricate European detailing on the walls and ceiling that had been retained during the remodel.

Kate leaned back on her shiny red leather bar stool with her legs crossed. "Memorable for the fake jewelry heist or for the fact that the police had to shut down the whole thing only an hour into it?"

"I had a bride in mid-updo when they cleared out the room." Fern shook his head and took a sip of his dirty martini. "Some poor girl is walking around with half her hair done up and the other half hanging out."

"If you ask me, it happened in the nick of time." Richard swirled the ice in his rocks glass. "A mother of the bride had almost talked me into a buffet themed around her Precious Moments figurines."

I pushed the two canvas tote bags filled with our leftover

show props underneath a bar stool Kate had saved for me and hopped up. The bar was crowded with brides who'd been exiled from the show but who didn't want to go home, and I felt lucky that we'd snagged a corner of the bar. I peered down the length of the lobby and noted that bridal show attendees occupied all the contemporary armless chairs and ornate French-inspired settees that made up the furniture vignettes throughout the room. The ones who weren't sitting were standing, some swaying close to the massive Grecian urns topped with ball topiaries.

I ordered a gin and tonic and saw an expression of surprise and pleasure cross Kate's face. Usually I'd have been the first one to be heading home instead of bellying up to the bar, but I hadn't seen Detective Reese since he'd left with Lorinda, and I'd promised him that I wouldn't leave.

"Cheers to the oddest bridal show ever," I said once my cocktail arrived. After we clinked glasses, I asked Kate, "Did our bartenders escape unscathed?"

"I snuck them out the loading dock. Two shirtless men wouldn't have made it five feet in this crowd." She gestured to the inebriated women around us. I didn't remind her that part of the reason the women were so tipsy in the first place might be our bar-themed booth.

"Should I ask what happened to their shirts?" I said.

Kate took a sip of her cocktail. "Suffice it to say that a few brides got overly excited and the shirts got damaged in the melee."

"Basically, the women ripped their shirts off?" I asked.

"In a nutshell, yes," Kate said. "Who knew engaged women could be so wild?"

Richard gave a small shudder and drained his glass. "I think you mean terrifying."

"Just because someone wants to serve local wine does not make them terrifying," I told him.

"Agree to disagree," Richard said.

"I don't know about the rest of you." Fern nibbled on an olive. "But today has restored my faith in bridal shows."

"We were shut down," I said. "And vendors were arrested. "

Fern nodded. "Wasn't it the most fun you've had in ages? I wish we hung out like this all the time."

"You're only saying that because you got to drink, watch our hunky bartenders, and shake a girl's head until diamonds fell out," I said.

"Exactly." Fern winked at me. "If I could shake some of our brides' heads like that I'd be in heaven."

Richard scanned the crowd. "Are Buster and Mack still downstairs?"

"The branches are harder to take down than they were to put up." I sipped my gin and tonic. "Plus, the police needed samples as evidence, so I doubt they'll be done for a while."

"Having the police at our event breakdowns is starting to become a very bad habit," Kate said.

I wagged a finger at her. "Technically, a bridal show isn't a wedding so it doesn't count."

"You keep telling yourself that, Annabelle," Richard said. "But how many other planners have a detective on speed dial?"

"Speaking of other wedding planners." And detectives. I let my eyes wander around the lobby. "What happened to Brianna? I saw her when we started to break down, but then she disappeared."

Kate shrugged. "Who knows? I'm surprised she isn't here at the bar passing out business cards."

"Wasn't our hot detective questioning her?" Fern asked.

"Reese?" I said. "You saw him questioning Brianna after the show?"

Fern plucked an olive out of his martini glass. "Very intensely if you ask me."

I took a gulp of my gin and tonic. So much for waiting for Reese. I bet he'd forgotten all about telling me not to leave the second Brianna batted her eyelashes at him. And I'd probably imagined the spark I'd felt between us and read too much into his actions. When it came down to it, he'd still never made a move. I felt a wave of irritation at myself for getting my hopes up again. I drained my glass and stood. "I think I'm going to head out."

"What?" Kate said. "I thought you promised to hang out with us and debrief."

"She did finish her drink," Fern said. "That's a first."

"I'm sorry." I scooped the tote bags from the floor. "But it's been a long day."

"You can say that again." Richard kissed me on both cheeks. "Call me later."

I nodded and then gave Fern an air kiss, trying to ignore his pout. My heels clicked on the black-and-white-tile lobby floor as I made my way to the valet parking stand on F Street, which was as crowded with brides as the bar. I fished my valet ticket from my bag and gave it to the nearest attendant.

"You might as well wait inside," he said. "It's going to be at least ten minutes."

Great. I went back inside and ducked into a side room off the lobby with a cluster of black leather and metal slope-backed chairs. The walls were covered in a paper that made it appear that the room had floor-to-ceiling bookshelves. Uber-chic hotels didn't have walls of books, I reminded myself. They had wallpaper that made it seem like you were surrounded by walls of books.

The room was tucked away enough that it was free from brides, so I set my bags on the floor and sank into a chair to wait, closing my eyes to avoid looking at the concentric prism pattern on the brown and beige carpet and enjoying the relative quiet.

"I thought you promised not to run off."

My eyes snapped open to find Detective Reese standing in front of me.

"Me?" I stood up, the gin and tonic giving me more courage than usual. "You're the one who disappeared."

He angled his head at me. "It took longer than I expected to question Ms. Goodman and her niece."

"So they were in on it together?" Curiosity overpowered my irritation.

Reese nodded. "It was pretty clever. Ms. Goodman planted the fake rings in her niece's hair before the blackout, and then the girl shut off the power while her aunt dumped the real rings into the vase and acted like a burglar had made off with them."

"So they planned for the fake rings to be discovered?"

"Apparently the plan included setting up the hairdresser. The model could claim innocence, and they could make off with the real diamonds after the show ended."

"And then report them as fakes afterward?" I asked.

"And claim they hadn't noticed in the chaos of the show," Reese said.

"Good thing Fern can spot a fake gemstone at a hundred paces."

Reese gave me a half smile. "Your friends do have their uses."

"Please." Now it was my turn to cross my arms. "You never could have cracked this case without us."

Reese stepped closer to me. "It wouldn't have been so hard if you hadn't sent me on a wild goose chase."

"Wild goose chase?" This was some gratitude considering I'd solved his case for him.

"The eyewitness who claimed to have heard the burglar run past her?"

I rolled my eyes. "Brianna? Don't blame me for that one. And it's not like you seemed to mind questioning her."

Reese unfolded his arms from across his chest. "What are you talking about?"

I felt my face flush. "Never mind. It's none of my business who you like."

Reese shook his head. "For your information, I spent the past fifteen minutes reading her the riot act for giving a false police report and impeding an investigation. Do you really think I'd like someone like that?"

I opened my mouth but shut it again, not sure how to respond. It made me happier than I wanted to admit that Brianna got in trouble with the police and even happier that Reese didn't like her.

"For someone who's pretty good at uncovering clues, you can be pretty clueless," he said.

Before I could revel in Reese admitting I had crime-solving skills or react to being called clueless, he leaned down and slipped one hand around my waist and flattened it into the small of my back. My irritation melted as I pressed against him.

"I'd say it's very much your business who I like," he whispered into my ear, his mouth brushing against my earlobe and sending shivers down my spine.

I gripped the back of the nearest chair to keep my quivering knees from buckling. If I'd been in any state to speak, I would have told Reese that, for once, I agreed with him.

Sign up for the author's mailing list and get a free copy of the first Annabelle Archer novel, Better Off Wed, winner of the Agatha Award for Best First Novel! Plus, you'll be the first to know about special deals and giveaways.

Get started by clicking the link below:

freebook.lauradurham.com

Review To a Kill

Chapter One

"This rain is going to ruin the view of the White House." I threw open one of the french doors that led to the Hay-Adams Hotel's narrow balcony overlooking both Lafayette Park and the most famous address in Washington, DC.

The gray clouds that hung over the city had been sending a steady mist of rain since the morning and, as it was now midafternoon, my hopes for a sunny wedding day, along with my hopes for a happy bride, were dwindling fast. I stepped onto the balcony and let the fine droplets settle on my skin. I breathed in the fresh scent of rain and felt glad it had washed away the pollen haze that had been hanging over the city for the past week, even if it did have to happen on the one day I needed clear skies. I ignored the clattering noise of the wedding band setting up behind me and took a moment to soak in the relative peacefulness of standing nearly ten stories above the city on a sleepy, rainy Saturday.

I reached into the pocket of my dress and felt for the packet of gummi bears my assistant, Kate, had given me earlier in the day. I popped a few into my mouth and savored the sugar rush. They were probably the only calories I'd get until much later that night so I didn't feel guilty about them. I held up the Cellophane candy packet to Buster, one half of my floral designing duo, and jiggled it.

He shook his head, pulling at his brown goatee with his fingers. "I'm too stressed to eat right now."

"Don't worry. It might clear up," I said, dropping the candy back into my pocket and patting Buster on his thick tattooed arm. I didn't fully believe what I said but, as the owner of Wedding Belles, one of DC's top wedding-planning companies, I'd learned that is was crucial to keep my creative team positive on the wedding day. Even if that meant lying to them.

Buster raised his eyebrows and the motorcycle goggles he wore on his forehead followed. "It's hard to pull off a springtime in Paris theme when it looks like a hurricane's brewing outside."

"Don't you think you're exaggerating a bit?"

Buster was usually the more even-keeled half of the floral design duo from Lush. His partner, Mack, was equally tattooed and leather-clad with a dark red goatee instead of a brown one but, generally speaking, the more emotional of the pair. I hoped Buster's nerves didn't mean that Mack was in a full-scale meltdown.

I turned from the view to look for Mack and glanced over the ballroom that had been transformed into springtime in Paris. One of the biggest selling points for holding a wedding at the Top of The Hay, the name for the iconic hotel's rooftop ballroom, was the two walls of glass french doors that wrapped around the L-shaped room and provided both natural light and a stunning view. It was the perfect pick for a bride wanting any type of garden theme, and it had been a natural fit for our bride who wanted to recreate Paris in the spring. Whitewashed Eiffel Towers were interspersed between the towering arrangements of pink tulips on a runner of grass that extended the length of the long, rectangular tables. A tiny easel sat at the top of each place setting with a guest's name painted over a pastel impressionist background, and white ladder-backed chairs wore pale-pink tulle skirts.

"There you are," I said as I spotted Mack walking toward us under the hanging flower garden that Buster had installed in the ceiling alcove over the dance floor.

Mack dodged a hanging tulip. "Well, I delivered the bride's bouquet."

"And?" I asked, not sure if I wanted to know the bride's reaction.

Mack flopped down in a nearby chair. "Let's just say that if I cursed, now would be the time I'd pick some choice words about our bride."

I cringed. Mack and Buster were members of a Christian biker gang, and I'd never heard a swear word leave their lips.

Buster closed the french doors. "She didn't like the collar of nerines around the tulips?"

"Who knows what she hated more?" Mack tugged at a loose thread on his black leather vest. "She said it gave her a headache."

"The scent of it?" I asked. "I thought you specifically chose flowers with no scent."

"I did," Mack said. "She approved every flower in the whole wedding, remember?"

"How could I forget?" I recalled every painstaking moment of the planning ordeal with Tricia, from bringing blooms to her house for her to sniff test to sending her MP3 files of every song the band played so she could eliminate songs that were in a key she found irritating to having the chef forward her the ingredient list for every bite that would be served so she could identify offending foods.

"So she's not going to carry it down the aisle?" Buster asked.

"She's not going to walk down the aisle." Kate stood in the open doorway across from us, her hands on her hips and the toe of one high heel thumping on the carpet.

I closed my eyes and dropped my head for a second. "Not this again."

"Yep. She claims the stress has made her too sick to attend her own wedding." Kate strode across the room, her blond bob bouncing with each step. She had long legs that she preferred to show to their full advantage with short skirts, even on a wedding day, so her fitted black dress stopped several inches north of her knees. When she reached Mack, she sat in the chair next to him, crossing her legs so that her dress rose even higher on her thighs.

"How can she be stressed?" I asked. "We've done everything for her."

"Beats me." Kate shrugged. "But I never understood all the syndromes she claims to have."

Buster held up one finger. "There's the hypersensitivity to light."

"And migraines brought on by the scent of lilies," Mack said. "And garden roses and peonies and lily of the valley."

Kate snapped her fingers. "And don't forget that anything louder than a speaking voice can make her swoon."

"Why is she having a wedding in the first place?" Buster asked. "It's filled with all the things she claims make her sick."

"I'm sympathetic to the girl if she really has all these problems," Mack said. "I know what it's like to get a migraine. But her symptoms seem to come and go."

Kate lowered her voice. "She's an attention whore. Why else would you be such a hypochondriac?"

Mack swatted at her. "Language, young lady."

Kate rubbed her arm where Mack had made contact. "Sorry, but I stand by my assessment. Annabelle and I caught her doing one of those Insanity workout DVDs when she claimed to be too exhausted to get out of bed."

"It's true," I said. "She cancelled one of our first meetings so we decided to drop her welcome box off at her house as a surprise."

"The surprise was us catching a glimpse of her working out like a maniac through a gap in her front curtains." Kate shook her head. "I knew she couldn't look as buff as she does by staying in bed all the time."

"Did you call her on it?" Buster asked.

"No. We mentioned it to her mother but she said that Tricia was in therapy to work through her hypochondria and need for attention and that we shouldn't say anything or it would make it worse."

"Worse than this?" Buster's motorcycle goggles lifted with his eyebrows.

Kate touched Buster's thick forearm. "That's what I said."

"Since she's a rich hypochondriac who needs a lot of attention, her mother thought the wedding would actually help," I said. "What better way to get more attention than a big wedding?"

"Not if you don't show up for it," Mack said.

I shook my head. "I'm sure she's bluffing."

"She probably needs some of the patented Annabelle Archer Zen," Kate said. She loved to tease me about being able to calm down even the most nervous brides just by being around them. So far, though, Tricia Toker had pushed the limits of even my Zen energy.

I sighed and mentally steeled myself for the bride's histrionics. "I'll go check on her. Fern should be done with everyone's hair by now."

"Fern is not done because Fern can't work under these conditions." The hairstylist to Washington's most elite, and all of our brides, stood in the doorway of the ballroom with a can of hairspray in one hand and a round brush in the other. Since Fern always tried to dress to the theme of the wedding, he wore a navy and white striped boatneck T-shirt with white pants and a navy beret. I noticed that his beret had slipped from its earlier jaunty tilt, and strands of dark hair had escaped from his low ponytail. He threw his brush on the floor. "Fern quits."

Buy *Review To a Kill* to continue reading . . .

ALSO BY LAURA DURHAM

Read the entire Annabelle Archer Series in order:

Better Off Wed

For Better Or Hearse

Dead Ringer (novella)

Review To A Kill

Death On The Aisle

Night of the Living Wed (novella)

Eat, Prey, Love

Groomed For Murder

Wed or Alive

To get notices whenever I release a new book, follow me on BookBub:

https://www.bookbub.com/profile/laura-durham

Did you enjoy this book? You can make a big difference!

I'm very lucky to have a loyal bunch of readers, and honest reviews are the best way to help bring my books to the attention of new readers.

If you enjoyed *Dead Ringer*, I would be very grateful if you could spend just five minutes leaving a review (it can be as short as you like) on the book's page on Goodreads, BookBub, or your favorite retailer.

Thanks for reading and reviewing!

ABOUT THE AUTHOR

Laura Durham has been writing for as long as she can remember and has been plotting murders since she began planning weddings in Washington, DC over twenty years ago. Her first novel, BETTER OFF WED, won the Agatha Award for Best First Novel.

When she isn't writing or wrangling brides, Laura loves traveling with her family, standup paddling, perfecting the perfect brownie recipe, and reading obsessively.

I'd love to hear from you! Find me at:
www.lauradurham.com
laura@lauradurham.com

ACKNOWLEDGMENTS

It's nice to return to the world of Annabelle Archer after a bit of a hiatus. I never completely left the mystery world, though, and want to send a shout-out to my friends at Mystery Writers of America (especially Margery Flax) for keeping me in the game. And virtual hugs to all the readers who emailed me and told me how much you loved the books and wanted more. Thank you!

Sincere thanks to Barb Goffman and Tim Jungr for their invaluable feedback and editing. Much gratitude to my dear husband who helped me with many of the technical aspects of reviving the Annabelle Archer series.

Copyright © 2017 by Broadmoor Books, LLC

Published by Broadmoor Books, LLC

Wake Forest, North Carolina

Cover Design by Alchemy Book Covers

CPSIA information can be obtained
at www.ICGtesting.com
Printed in the USA
LVHW091741120120
643360LV00008B/1215/P

9 780999 149430